THINGS
DON'T
BREAK

THINGS DON'T BREAK

STORIES BY
Richard Rosenbaum

TIGHTROPE BOOKS

Tightrope Books
#207-2 College Street,
Toronto Ontario, Canada M5G 1K3
tightropebooks.com
bookinfo@tightropebooks.com

EDITOR: Deanna Janovski
COVER IMAGE: David Jang
COVER & LAYOUT DESIGN: David Jang

Produced with the assistance of the Canada Council for the Arts and the
Ontario Arts Council.

Library and Archives Canada Cataloguing in Publication

Rosenbaum, Richard, 1979-, author
    Things don't break / Richard Rosenbaum.

Short stories.
ISBN 978-1-988040-19-6 (softcover)

    I. Title.

PS8635.06497T45 2017   C813'.6   C2017-902190-7

Table of Contents

I Don't Believe in You

SHE COMES IN THE ROOM LIKE HAMLET'S FATHER, EXCEPT NAKED, and ruins everything. My eyes are closed, so I can only hear her. And that's the problem. Her hair is twisting up in little U-shaped curls, and I know because that's just what it tends to do in the mornings. The bedroom door creaks open loud as fucking Armageddon, and she comes sidling up next to me and just completely shatters any appearance of calm I'm trying to maintain. I haven't slept all night. I've been working. Not that she understands that. Her smell, the smell of peaches or something, gets stronger and stronger, and then her hand is on the back of my neck. I'm trying not to notice.

She says something that sounds like a badger in a microwave during mating season. Probably real words, could have been "You've been sitting here all night" or "It's freezing in this house" or "Madness is just fear and indecision." But I'm trying really hard not to listen. My senses have been functioning in some unusual frequencies lately. I really wish she would go away. I'm right in the middle of something here. And I tell her so.

She doesn't get it. She doesn't know how important this is right now. At three in the morning on a midsummer night, there are some things that are just so much more critical than avenging dead relatives. She takes her hand off the back of my neck and moves away, just not far enough. The residue of her DNA can remain on my skin for weeks after she touches me sometimes. All her perfectly manicured, carefully perfumed little X chromosomes are trying to burrow their way into my skull again, as usual, but I've already taken care of that, so I'm not concerned. Just annoyed.

I say some words that probably sound like "Go back to sleep," although what I mean by them is "I only wish anything could be as important as you think I am."

"Momentum equals force times acceleration," I say, but I guess it sounds more like "I don't think this is working out."

I have no idea what she's on about now. Something clearly too personal for me to have any interest in. If it's got nothing to do with mentally training the capillaries in my head to increase the blood flow to the nerves of my inner ear, I just couldn't care less at the moment. I'm starving, too. I think it would be lovely if she'd make me some eggs. But instead she goes and turns the radio completely off, and I totally lose it. I mean I just snap. This experiment is so over now; she shot it in the brain the second she entered the room. I just can't imagine what she's thinking about, I really can't.

I say, "I've been turning down the volume on that radio by one-tenth every twenty minutes for the last eight hours, my love, and I was almost finished with it." I say it slowly. I say it with venom. But what I really mean by it is so appalling that the words do not exist that could express the sentiment accurately.

I don't even know where she is anymore. Her utter lack of morbid self-obsession was beginning to get to me, quite honestly. Something is happening, but I can't tell if it's a car door slamming or me repeatedly banging my head on the table until I'm unconscious.

Things Don't Break

PEOPLE ALWAYS ASK ME ABOUT VINCENT VAN GOGH. EVERYTHING I know about that man I learned from random people on the street coming up to me and asking. Nineteenth-century expressionist painter. Epileptic. One time during a seizure, he went nuts and cut his ear off and mailed it to some prostitute or something.

Is that what happened? No. Is that what you did? No. Do you have epilepsy? No. Cancer. You idiot.

A lovely midsummer's day, sun shining, birds singing. I'm walking down this street, so familiar even though I haven't been here for close to three years now. Head hanging low between my shoulders. I pull a little folded-up scrap of paper out of my pocket. A napkin, actually. On one side is the name, address, phone number, website, and logo of a restaurant I used to go to. On the other side is written, in fading blue ink, in her handwriting, a date, today's date.

I'm just going down the sidewalk, the city continuing to function municipally all around me. To my right, the people don't even notice me. To my left, everyone is staring.

Almost there and this can't be good, won't be good, I know it. I'm approaching the restaurant, and I feel like I'm walking down death row. Electrocution. Lethal injection. I'm sitting in the restaurant, across from her, saying goodbye. The last time for three years. Firing squad. I'm sitting in the doctor's office waiting room. The doctor comes out, small steps, looks down at me sitting there, with a grave expression on his face, tears about to break out all over mine. Crucifixion.

Stop. My gaze rises, from my shoelaces it ascends, up, up to the sign that clearly shows that I've arrived at the Galaxy Diner.

Except it isn't. It doesn't say that. There is no sign. Well, there is a sign, but just not that one, not the one I expected to be there.

Now I'm staring, incredulous. I look back down at the napkin, and then back up at the sign again. Number forty-two. This is definitely the place. Except it isn't.

So I'm standing in front of the ex-Galaxy Diner, shifting from one foot to the other. She's sitting across from me, empty cup of coffee, and she's writing a date, today's date, a day precisely three years from today, on the back of a napkin. Then she's going to the bathroom. You don't expect this kind of thing. You never think that your plans for the future will be foiled by the Galaxy Diner going out of business. I'm going to sleep just like everyone else, and I'm waking up like Vincent van Gogh, one step closer to that psychopath from *Apocalypse Now*, the one with the necklace. You just don't anticipate it, you don't make contingency plans for, okay, what if your favourite restaurant becomes a carpet store? You forget all about change, you forget that time keeps happening, even if you decide to have no part of it, even if you decide that you're not getting any older, dammit. Time still happens, even if you refuse to grow up.

And so, standing there gawking stupidly, as there's no non-stupid way in which to gawk, really, at the sign on the store—and then there's a voice standing behind me, and the first thing that it says is "You grew your ... " and I'm turning around to face it, and now the voice is saying, " ... hair ... oh God."

Yes, you'd be surprised at how badly long hair hides a missing ear, you really would. It works all right if you're not moving at all, not even turning around to look at the curiously unfamiliar face of someone important, someone you haven't seen for so long that you were beginning to wonder if she was ever real at all. And those Elmer Fudd hunting hats with the ear flaps just look bloody ridiculous, especially in the summer.

"Yeah," I say, "and you cut yours. Your hair. Hi."

"Hi," she says, seeming distracted. God knows why. "I'm leaving," she says. "I'm going to Europe for I don't know how long." She says, "What happened to you?"

"Nothing, leaky cellphone," I say. I say, "I'm going to die, aren't I? Am I going to die?" and the doctor is shaking his head clinically. "It's a carpet store," I say, indicating the Galaxy Diner.

"So it is," she says. "Well then, it's a carpet store." She's ordering a large double-double. I'm ordering a large lemon tea with two sugars and a lemon cranberry muffin. The doctor is ordering additional radiological investigation. I'm ordering myself not to cry. "Do you need any carpets?"

And recent scientific studies indicate that we're sitting together on a rolled-up carpet; ostensibly there's no connection between cellular phone use and ear cancer, but these kinds of tumours are often more extensive than clinically apparent if you ask me, and if you're talking all the time then you're never thinking, are you?

"How was Europe?" I ask. "Tell me everything. What are my chances? I want the truth." She's bouncing nervously up and down on the carpet.

"I'll be back," she says. "I'll meet you right here, in exactly three years." I can't find comfort in anything anymore. She says, "It was great, beautiful. In Italy I kicked the Arch of Titus." A sleeve resection and a skin graft are occasionally possible for early lesions but have limitations related to the ill-defined boundaries of the tumour, and surgery may be incomplete. She says, "In Ireland I made a little boat out of newspaper and watched it float down the Liffey."

"If you ask me," I say, "they should *tell you* that the prosthetic can cause an allergic reaction." I say, "What am I supposed to do now?" She's paying for my muffin and sliding the napkin across the table to me, looking doleful.

"I'm sorry," she says. "I'm sorry," the doctor says. "In Spain I visited the town where the Communists killed all the Anarchists in the civil war, even though they were on the same side," she says.

The carpets all smell like chemicals. She smells like violets. The manager is looking at us askance. She smells like violets. Everyone is staring. If you ask me, it's all about entropy. All around us, time is happening. Studies won't indicate this, but it's true: sometimes the only cure for boredom is mutation. A lateral temporal bone resection or subtotal temporal bone resection may be necessary in order to remove the tumour completely. "I know you'll be fine," someone says, I don't know who. External X-ray megavoltage beam irradiation is quite often indicated in view of the closeness of the surgical margin of resection. Synchrony means never having to say you're sorry. I say,

"Why is this happening?"

She says, "It's important for me to get out and see the world for myself." She says, "So what, um, have you been doing?" Treatment volume is designed to cover the potential areas of involvement while minimizing unnecessary irradiation to the adjacent vital organs (eye and brain). Treatment is usually prescribed postoperatively. She's getting up. She's leaving. She's leaving. "I have to go," she says. "It was really great to see you again." Time keeps happening. "We'll see each other again soon, I promise," she says. And time keeps on happening, all around us.

"I keep it in a jar in my bedroom," I say.

She says, "Ew, you're kidding!"

"Of course I'm kidding." Of course I'm not kidding.

I'm sitting, alone, in the Galaxy Diner, in the radiology ward, on a carpet. And time keeps happening, time continues to happen, even if you decide that you're never getting over it.

Chicken Coup

SUNDAY AFTERNOON AND YOU'RE SITTING AT A TABLE AT THAT FRIED chicken place while those radical animal rights people are busy interrupting family meals by distributing paper buckets filled with blood and bones to screaming children.

While you somewhat sympathize with the parents, who, after all, are just trying to get some protein into their little darlings after soccer practice, albeit deep-fried protein (though the restaurant chain has surreptitiously removed the word *fried* from their name, since explicitly fried foods are now considered indecorous in polite society), you're more amused than anything else. You've always found the actions of this particular group kind of arbitrary, more like pretentious performance art or low-grade terrorism than righteous consciousness-raising. Questionable at best. But you're actually quite enjoying the reactions of all parties involved: the activists' rabid, mad-eyed cavorting, sloshing blood all over the place and throwing paper airplanes made from pamphlets that illustrate the hellish conditions under which your lunch was raised; the children screaming, running around (appropriately enough) like chickens with their heads cut off, trying to avoid getting blood thrown on them and occasionally taking a particularly sharp paper airplane to the eye; the parents also shrieking, attempting simultaneously to pacify their brood while fending off the militant hippies. You can almost hear the kids' little minds snapping like wishbones, bringing about nostalgic memories of your own beloved childhood traumas. The restaurant staff are vastly outgunned and outnumbered, utterly unprepared for an incident of this magnitude, and most of them are cowering in the kitchen waiting for the police to arrive.

You're munching on a wing and internally composing a response just in case any of the activists decide to come over and accost you too (you're planning to mention that, to the best of your knowledge, your leather jacket had, in life, been a vegan) when yet another group of pissed-off antagonists enters the establishment.

There's about half a dozen of them, around six feet tall. Their gigantic Doc Marten boots have obviously been specially made for their bony three-toed feet, and many of the feathers on their wings and necks have been plucked, revealing some quite frightening tattoos on the naked flesh underneath. The combs and wattles (those things on the tops and bottoms of their heads, respectively) are an angry, bright red. They're all wearing leather jackets, adorned with swastika armbands.

The parents and their children are visibly horrified; the animal rights people seem elated.

The leader of the activists (she of green hair and Birkenstocks) goes up to the apparent leader of the mutant chicken gang with wide eyes and a wide smile.

"I can't believe you're here!" she coos, obsequiously. "We've been fighting for your rights for—"

Her words are cut short by the head rooster.

"Shut the fuck up, bitch," he crows, and then backhands (back-wings?) her across the face, sending her sprawling athwart the floor, blood exploding from her nose. New screams erupt from the crowd. All hell breaks loose as now the parents are jumping through windows to create alternate escape routes (the chickens are blocking the main doors), the children are screaming and wetting themselves, either running after their mommies or scared catatonic, and the activists are trying to protect themselves from the rampaging poultry, the rights of whom they had so recently been trying to protect. You're just sitting there. The kids and their parents don't appear to be the targets of the chickens' unholy wrath; only the animal rights people seem to have that honour. Within minutes, the chickens have rendered the hippies a gory and largely unconscious pile in the middle of the restaurant floor.

The chickens' leader grabs the last of the activists by his shirt-collar and dumps him unceremoniously on the top of the pile. Before losing consciousness, the activist croaks out a single strangled word:

"Why?"

You'd never heard a chicken laugh contemptuously before, but just now you do.

"Those ads youse guys did a few months ago," he says, "comparing chicken coops to concentration camps. You remember?"

The activist nods. The chicken concludes his explanation: "We ain't got nuthin' in common with no Jews."

Drawn and Quartered

IT WAS ONCE THE CASE THAT HANGING WAS AMONG THE WORST FATES a person could suffer; you murdered someone, or you raped someone, or maybe you stole someone's chicken and happened to be very unlucky, and if you got caught, they would hang you. The execution method of choice for some of the most heinous acts imaginable: "For your crime," the judge would pronounce, "you are sentenced to be hanged by the neck until you are dead." Even in many places where capital punishment is still practised, hanging has been outlawed as excessively cruel and unusual.

Today, hanging by the neck until dead is what a teenage boy does one day after school when he's horny and bored.

Right now, M. is also hanging. Not by her neck, and she will still be alive when they lower her again. It's true that her feet aren't touching the ground, but hers is as much a suspension of disbelief as anything else.

"You are absolutely free," proclaims a tiny girl with an astonishing, authoritative voice. "You are responsible for nothing, beholden to no one," she screams at M., who is the centre of attention on this particular night. The room is dark, stark, and crowded, sweaty yet scrupulously sanitized. A single light bulb hangs from a chain in the middle of the ceiling, and closer to the wall hangs M., hovering like an angel, trying to scream and also not to scream. Trying to hold her blood in. "You are *radically* free, a free radical!" shouts the small girl with the big voice, the organizer, over the din of the crowd— dozens of people have assembled this evening to witness tonight's event. "You created yourself! You can do anything! So why shouldn't you do everything?"

Inside M., something unconscious squirms.

It was once the case, before, let's say, the middle of the twentieth century, that permanent body modifications were the exclusive country of outlaws. Who had tattoos in Western society? Ex-convicts and pirates, or occasionally those persons deemed unacceptable by the state for reasons those individuals could not control or change, even if they had wanted to.

Today: look around the room, examine M.'s admirers and gawkers, that screaming, sweating mass, and try to find someone without a rose on their chest, barbed wire or flames around their arm, a butterfly on their ankle, a skull on their shoulder and/or hieroglyphs at the base of their spine. Go ahead and try. Seriously. Take your time.

And while this is all taking place, remember, M. still has no idea. How could she?

It was once the case that flagellation was the preferred form of punishment for those criminals whose crimes were not deemed sufficiently serious to merit the death penalty.

In ancient times, the Jewish court would administer a maximum of thirty-nine lashes to a person found guilty of various offenses; a doctor would be present to supervise the punishment, and if the pain became too much for the person to bear, it would be ended early. In addition, if the person wet himself during his flagellation, the remainder of the lashes would be withheld, his humiliation deemed sufficient chastisement in itself. The ancient Romans, on the other hand, would often flagellate a prisoner with a metal-tipped whip before crucifying him, though someone afflicted thus sometimes bled to death before he could even be taken to the cross. In colonial Australia, British criminals were sometimes condemned to more than three thousand lashes, though if the offender passed out from blood loss before all of his lashes were administered, the remainder of his punishment could be put off until he had sufficiently healed; sometimes this could stretch out over a period of months or even years.

Two of the primary tools for dispensing this penalty were the bullwhip (consisting of a wooden handle attached to a single thong made of leather) and the cat-o'-nine-tails (similar, but with nine thongs made from braided rope, sometimes with metal balls or barbs attached to the tips of the thongs).

Today, both of these implements, along with many other varieties of torture devices, are available at the sex shop around the corner.

What's happening to M. is technically called "suicide suspension," though that's kind of a misnomer: she's not actually attempting to kill herself. It's just that the position of her body under these conditions appears similar to someone hanging from a noose. She's not doing it for herself, really. It's actually for the spectators. This is recreation. It's not sexual; it's entertainment. Like watching a movie or a baseball game. She's a performer. An *artist*.

Six stainless-steel fish hooks are currently embedded in M.'s skin—one in each shoulder, one on each side of the back, and one in each hip—attached with parachute line tied in figure-eight knots to the suspension frame that is holding her aloft. First she was punctured with regular piercing needles, and only then were the hooks inserted, so she could be hoisted up to bear her own weight before her captivated audience.

This isn't the first time she's done it. Usually, once she's perforated, at first she'll feel a strong tugging where the hooks dig into her skin, which dissolves into a feeling of surrender as her body leaves the ground. In time, she'll have a sensation of euphoric floating, sometimes entering an almost trance-like state. There's no noise; there's no pain. She's alone in the universe and completely at peace.

Not this time. This time, something seems to have gone kind of wrong, though she doesn't want anyone else to know it. It's not smart, she's aware of that, but at the moment M. is hoping that she'll be able to recover and leave her audience satisfied. She doesn't want to come down.

But it *hurts*. A metaphor would be superfluous here: *there are razor-sharp metal hooks puncturing her skin, and she's hanging from them*. They're not spinning her around, but they might as well be. The last time she felt this ill was when she had the chicken pox at age ten, and her mother stuck her in an ice-cold bath to reduce her fever. If she were to vomit, it would be on herself, all over her trembling, naked body. She may lose consciousness. She's just not sure.

Only later, when it's already too late, will M. find out. And the father, he will never know. She'll never tell him.

Was this why it happened? Does it matter? Fortunately, tonight is all about a woman's right to never have to choose.

It was once the case that a person convicted of treason in England would be subjected to a punishment called "drawing and quartering," which consisted of being dragged on a hurdle to the execution site, hanged by a noose but taken down before death, disemboweled—with the intestines and genitals set on fire in front of the victim while still alive—and finally beheaded and cut into four roughly equal pieces. Often the quartered body and the decapitated head would be displayed separately throughout the town to discourage other potential traitors.

Someday soon, you will be able to pay someone to do this to you. Just wait and see.

M. is oblivious to everything but the pain, the pain making her forget, forget the whole world. The sphere of her sensation includes nothing but her own body. It hurts so much that she can't remember that she has a soul at all. And, you know, maybe that's even kind of the whole point.

The Fence

EVERY MORNING BEFORE WORK, CARRIE DURNING WALKS HER DOG IN the park down the street from her house. Iggy the golden retriever is now twelve years old, only weeks younger than Carrie's child, Andrea (Andy), and besides some mild arthritis and a bit of a weight problem, is in remarkably good health for a dog his age. When Andy was born, her father, Carrie's husband, insisted that they had to have a dog as well. A child needs a dog, he reasoned. Even more than good parenting, a dog was the best, most surefire way to teach a child how to love and be loved. His parents had never let him own a dog growing up, and he firmly believed that this was the main reason for his intimacy issues, which he and Carrie had worked on in couples therapy beginning surprisingly early into their marriage. Andy needed a dog or she would be forever stunted and incomplete. Carrie was not convinced. But she did let herself be dragged to the breeder a month before bringing little Andy home from the hospital, just to indulge her husband. There she fell instantly and irrevocably in love with a puppy whose fur was the exact same shade of blond that Carrie had been dyeing her hair since the summer before starting high school.

Andy's father still believes that a dog is essential to any child's mental health. Which is why he insisted that Carrie, and not he, keep Iggy when he left their family for a woman the same age Carrie was when the two of them first met at the festival commemorating the twenty-fifth anniversary of Woodstock.

When Carrie leaves the house in the morning sometime between five and six to take Iggy to the park, Andy is still asleep. When Mark was there it hadn't been a big deal, but once it was just Carrie and Andy, it became a bit of a problem. The dog had to be walked, and it couldn't wait until after Carrie came home from work, but she also didn't feel right about leaving her child all alone while she took Iggy to the park. The one time Carrie had planned just to run the dog around the backyard once Andy was off to school, Iggy had an unprecedented accident on the floor immediately outside the master bedroom in the middle of the night, which Carrie, bleary eyed and barefoot as she staggered to the bathroom that morning, encountered in a very unpleasant way. Carrie interpreted this as a sign that she should not even have considered disrupting Iggy's schedule, and while she didn't actually believe that the dog had somehow known what she had planned for the day, she did sort of feel sometimes this sympathetic, if not quite telepathic, pet/owner bond that made Iggy very sensitive to Carrie's thoughts and moods, and figured that she owed it to him not to mess with his life any more than was absolutely necessary. The poor thing had been traumatized enough by the departure of Mark, who had doted on him and fed him cheese things when Carrie wasn't looking. The cheese was a major contributor to Iggy's borderline obesity, which did not help his arthritis, which gave him an aversion to movement in general as he aged, making it even more important for him to get regular exercise.

Andy would often spurn the couch to lean up against Iggy in front of the television after school, a position Carrie would find them in when she came home from her job at the publishing company, where she copyedited high school history and geography textbooks. Andy's hair was also the same shade of yellow as Iggy's fur, their follicular issuances melding into each other as they lay there together on the living room floor. The mother had no clue where her daughter's blond-hair gene had come from, didn't think it was very likely that the peroxide had just slipped into her own DNA over twentyish years of scrupulous monthly colouring, but she was happy about it nonetheless because it meant that they got a lot of "You two look exactly the same!" when they went out together, which Carrie always felt was meant to be some kind of compliment on the quality or the strength of her genome if not explicitly on her actual parenting. But nobody had ever said that Andy resembled her father, which, to Carrie, was something, at least.

As for hiring a professional dog-walker, there were none who were willing to take Iggy out before sunrise, and anyway, what do you think that Carrie is made of money or something?

This morning it's the first of November and sadistically cold when Carrie puts the blue polyester collar around Iggy's fat, furry neck, wraps herself in her blue wool coat, and heads down the street to the park. When she reaches the park, she doesn't immediately understand what's happened: she finds it completely enclosed in a gateless chain-link fence that had certainly not been there the day before.

Carrie says, "What the hell?"—her first speech act that day—and then feels vaguely guilty about it and looks down at Iggy, who doesn't appear particularly offended by the expletive, or even especially concerned by the presence of the fence, for that matter. Carrie, though, is very concerned. This is her park. Not just hers, of course, everyone's. But hers no less than anyone else's. And more importantly, it is Iggy's park. Adding up the time she'd spent walking Iggy here, before coffee, before even the sun, she had left her child for a total of something like one hundred and eighty-two-and-a-half days just to come to this park. More than half a year, over one twenty-fourth of Andy's life, had been spent by her mother, and her dog of course, at this park. Carrie has never been strong in math, but this calculation disturbs her. Sure, Andy had been unconscious for all that time. But that isn't the point. It is the principle of the thing. Nobody has the right to deprive Carrie or Iggy or anyone of their access to the park's green grass or thin young maples or its round, still duck pond. For any reason. Who would do this? And why? How could anyone have such contempt for a poor, sweet old dog? Carrie begins to boil under her wool coat in the cold autumn morning.

Well, this is outrageous. Simply outrageous and intolerable, and Carrie will not stand for it.

"Don't worry," she tells Iggy. "I'll get you in there. I'll get us in."

The dog looks up at her and maybe raises his eyebrows like, seriously? But it's dark, so she can't be certain. She wraps the end of Iggy's leash through a link in the fence with the deathlike sound of chain clanking against chain, ties it into a loose knot. She pulls the membranous, black fake-suede gloves down over her wrists and tucks them into the sleeves of her coat. She reaches up, hooking the gloved fingers of both hands through two links above her head and placing the tip of one boot into a link six inches off the ground. Once Mark had left and she was on her own, she'd let her Climbing Club membership lapse—she just couldn't justify the expense anymore—but she had learned a few tricks. She knows how to get to the top of something and over the other side.

Nobody is around—nobody sensible and diurnal, anyway—but Carrie casts a circumspective glance behind her before beginning her ascent. She lifts herself up and up and up the same way she once saw a snake scale the side of a house when she was a child. It scared her to watch it then, and it scares her to imitate it now. Something unsettlingly real about the pure verticality, uncanny in a way that the safe, indoor climbing walls never were, those things specifically constructed to be mounted up by human bodies that were not materially built for travelling in such a counterintuitive direction. Her heart shouts, but her limbs remember, and she moves.

Upon reaching the top of the fence, she looks down and for a moment can't remember what she is doing there. Then she sees, dimly, the figure of Iggy looking back up at her from the grass, and it returns. She flips a leg over the top of the fence. It's not barbed or anything as complicated as that, but its peak is crowned with half-links of chain sticking up into the air like a string of antennae or a row of flowers. The inseam of her pants catches on one of these outcroppings, and when she flips her other leg over, she hears a distinctive tear, then feels a terrible chill.

She swears, then hopes that Iggy didn't hear her. Dogs have good hearing. They aren't nice pants or anything, just her old camo-print jeans, baggy from before she lost all that weight, blobbed irrevocably with butterfly-yellow paint from redecorating her daughter's bedroom. She needed new ones anyway; Andy was always saying so. And yet they were familiar and comfortable, and she hates to lose them, and she holds this fence personally responsible for their mutilation. Furious sweat scratches her scalp. Humiliation scorches her face. She does not believe her now-exposed thigh is bleeding, but cannot yet be sure. Too dark, too sweat-sticky. She may require a tetanus shot. Someone will pay for this.

Carefully she extricates herself and begins her descent. Probably faster than advisable. But she's growing more and more upset with the situation. She's losing her cool. Literally, figuratively. Her boots lock into one link after another, each lower than the last, down and down and down, and a bit less than a metre from the ground she just jumps.

Her ankle buckles, her foot turns sideways and goes horizontal to the ground. Not broken—it still moves—not even sprained, she's pretty sure, but it hurts, radiates pain and heat up her leg. Bruised, maybe. The sheer irresponsibility—of the police, the Department of Parks and Recreation, whoever it is. She practically foams with sulfurous anger, embarrassment. Conviction. Righteousness.

Time for all that later. Now there is a mission to accomplish.

In the dark, Carrie creeps along the edge of the park, along the inside of the fence. Keeping her weight off the hurt ankle. She makes eye contact with Iggy through the chain links. The dog regards her skeptically. It is an expression she recognizes. She has seen it before.

She reaches the corner of the fence, at the edge of the park. Stops. Where the hell did this thing come from?

Bending at the knees, gently, Carrie examines the spot where the two walls of the fence come together on the ground—though it is hard to see in the dark; the sun has only just barely hinted at rising, bruising the eastern sky a mauve convexity. The thing, the fence, she sees, is stable enough but not infrangible, obviously not intended to be permanent. Rather than line posts set into concrete to keep it standing, Carrie now notices that it's actually a bunch of individual panels of wire netting slammed together, and not all that securely. Something of a slapdash effort, Carrie muses, and she is suddenly very relieved that she didn't uproot the thing by climbing on it—she could have come away with a lot more than a bruised ankle. Or possibly not come away at all. Which, thinking about it, only makes her angrier: she could have *killed herself* up there! Who on earth would erect such a shoddy, ill-conceived enclosure? Besides the absence of a top rail, there's no bottom wire either, and only some kind of flexible, if durable, vinyl ribbon thing holding the panels together, not even tension bands. It's as if they, whoever they are, *want* people not only to get into the park despite the fence, but also to be injured or worse while doing it. The incompetence, the sheer arrogance of it. Some people might even regard the fence as an incentive, a challenge to be overcome. What's it called—an attractive nuisance. Doesn't anyone but her think about these things? Isn't there anyone in charge here? Or, more ominously, what if that's the whole point, what if the fence is some kind of a *trap*. She wouldn't put that past them.

Carrie straightens herself up and kicks at the bottom corner of the fence where the two panels meet. She wants to open it, yes, but now she wants to hurt it, too. It makes a sound like a bottle hitting the kitchen floor but failing to break. Iggy looks up. The panels separate just a little. Enough to encourage Carrie to continue. She kicks at it again. With the ball of her foot, the uninjured one, so she won't break all her toes inside the leather boot. She's not an idiot. The panels part a little further. Another kick, another couple of inches. Two more quick blows with the boot, then another, and now there's a distinct gap, an isosceles of absence large enough for a person to get through. Well, to crawl through. That ought to suffice.

As Carrie Durning gets down on her hands and knees in the frost-capped grass and squeezes herself, inch by inch, through her new rupture, she fully comprehends how ridiculous she must look. But she has no choice. Fortunately no one is watching. Except Iggy. Carrie drags herself through the hole, muddying her gloves, further staining her pants, wind pouring into the rip at her thigh. On the other side, the outside, she stands up again. She looks down at Iggy and says, "Don't look at me like that. I'm doing this for you." She unties the end of the leash from the fence and kneels back down, says, "Come on now," and squirms through the gap once more, this time with the retriever shuffling behind her uneagerly.

Inside now, the both of them. Carrie gets to her feet, leash in hand, triumphant. Finally the dog can have a shit in peace.

Dawn begins to burn in the distance. Limping, shivering, Carrie takes Iggy through the park along their customary spiral trail, their orbit declining till they reach the centre, the duck pond, which they circle once, then straight back out. As the sun gently rises, Carrie starts seeing things. The park is not familiar. It's different.

Broken pumpkins like smashed open heads, orange brains splattered over dead icteric grass.

Exploded eggs everywhere like hand grenades, white shell shrapnel, yellow splashes of spoiled potential.

Broken glass caltrops, shards of brown and green, sticky and almost imperceptible.

Naked trees mummified in toilet paper, humiliated blind and terrified, wrapped with the pulped and processed remains of their brethren.

Spray-painted obscenities swelling across every visible surface—the trees, the benches, the concrete paths and monuments. Random imprecations, different colours and styles of script arguing over each other about which race or culture ought to get out or to get fucked. Inartistic swastikas.

Iggy the golden retriever noses dubiously at the ground. Carrie Durning forgets to breathe. Nobody could stop this?

Then the smell.

As they get closer to the heart of the park, they stumble upon, huddled cultically around the spew of dross from overthrown trash bins, corpse upon corpse—squirrels, raccoons, sparrows and pigeons, even a cat or two—white foam bubbling from their every cold orifice, bodies swollen and contorted in echoes of agony. Not too far off, Carrie sees ducks floating upside-down at the lip of the pond. Her stomach rises as her heart falls, and when Iggy tries to investigate, Carrie shrieks like a demon.

Iggy jerks backward by his leash before Carrie realizes she's done it, but once she has she bolts for escape, dragging reluctant Iggy behind her. In her panic, in her rage, she can't consider cause and effect or sort out aggressors or defenders. These are no longer of concern. Something terrible has happened. Someone will suffer for it. Someone must. As long as it isn't her. That's all she knows.

The dog moves slowly.

The Oughts

2009.

Her hair that burnt-out crunchy orange that's the colour of attempting to remove all colour, like maple leaves on the ground in October. Oliver stares, follows it from the crown of her head, hanging stiff and stringy, down till its blunt end at the point of her chin.

"I booked us five days of recording time at the studio next week," the hair says. Well, the owner of the hair. Polly. "And if you don't get that guitar of yours fixed by then, I swear to fucking Apollo I will impale you through the lungs with it, do you hear me?"

Her lips thin, viscerally pink. Oliver's fingers strum idly, discordantly, at the strings of the guitar in question. Polly's eyes green and serious. Oliver's head nods, maybe at Polly's words, but maybe at the unheard beat of some imaginary drum, which only infuriates her further.

She must have broken up with him, he thinks. That's why the impatience. This is good news. Inside his head, Oliver flips the little kill switch connected to his brain's "crush on Polly" circuit, imagining hearing it click. When she's involved with someone there's no point, but when she's single Oliver can enjoy some nice unrequited longing.

"Everything okay?" he says. "You seem, like, upset." Inside him, Oliver's lungs expand in Polly's direction. Inflating, deflating.

"I am upset," she says, as if just getting the words out is a really exhausting task for her. "Because it is the year two thousand nine of the common era, and our band is called The Oughts, and the whole point of calling it that was to capitalize on the like zeitgeist of the first decade of the twenty-first century, and that decade is now nearly over, and we have no recordings that are not total shit, and we haven't ever made more than a hundred dollars playing a gig, and this is unacceptable!"

Oliver strums, looking really sort of understanding and friend-ish.

"You broke up with him, right?" His voice low with compassion; inside, a livid heart pumping.

"Fuck you," says Polly. Pulls her gloves down over her wrists as far as she can, her eyes leaving Oliver's. "Yes," she says.

"He was a dick anyway," Oliver says, which is not true. Oliver actually kind of liked this one.

"You're a dick," Polly says, "and I've had it with your dickitry. I'm serious about the guitar thing. Get it fixed. Or get a new one. I won't have that piece of crap crapping out on us in the middle of a studio session. Will you get it fixed?"

"You're right, you're right," Oliver says.

"Will you get it fixed?"

"I know, it needs fixing."

"Will you. Get it. Fixed."

"Okay, okay!"

"Say it. Say the words."

"I'll get it fixed!" He clutches it to himself like he's afraid she'll take it away from him. A sound like metal reverberates from its body into his ears.

"Promise?"

"I promise, I promise."

"Thank you."

Damn, Oliver thinks, but more with like admiration than resentment. She knows him well enough to know he'll never do anything unless she makes him promise to. And she only makes him promise things that are actually beneficial. This is one reason why they get along.

2002.

They meet in their last year of high school. Guitar class. Both of them in the front row.

The first day, before the teacher arrives, Oliver sits there with the standard-issue public school acoustic guitar in his lap, expending his full concentration on plonking out the bass line from "Come As You Are"—which is the only thing he knows how to play—over and over and over, like a needle in a scratched vinyl groove. He doesn't even notice when Polly takes the seat beside him.

"That's a good song," she says, alerting him to her presence. He stops playing and looks at her. He knows her by sight as that pretty girl who always has her guitar case, but they've never had any classes together and their circles of friends don't overlap, so they've never really spoken.

"Oh, thanks," he says, which is stupid, so then he says, "I mean, yeah, it is."

She's got her blue acoustic, wider at its widest point than her body is, and it's covered with stickers of bands that must be good because Oliver has never heard of them.

"Can you play any of the rest of that album?" she asks.

"Oh man, no way," he says. "This is literally the only thing I can even play at all. That's why I'm in this class, I want to learn."

"Gotcha," she says. "I'm in this class for the easy A. I've been playing since I was eleven. I can play anything." The way she says this, it doesn't come off as arrogant, just confident, self-aware, because it is clearly actually true.

"Nice," Oliver says. "I'm Oliver." He reaches out to shake her hand, and her bare hand reciprocates. Her fingers long, with blue polished nails.

"I'm P.J."

"What does that stand for?"

"Uh, Polly Jane. Everyone calls me P.J., though."

"I like Polly better," Oliver says. "Do you mind if I call you Polly?"

"No," Polly says, a little bewildered. "No, I don't mind."

2004.
Value Village is where they go to look for a guitar for Oliver, because

it's consistently the best place to get pretty much anything you want for unreasonably cheap, and also because "I got my guitar at Value Village" is an incredibly punk rock thing to be able to say when you're interviewed by Cokemachineglow or Stereogum or whatever. No Pitchfork, they swore (well, Polly made Oliver swear): never would they give an interview to Pitchfork, no matter how famous they got.

Musical instruments and electronics and such live at the back of the store, which is not, of course, a village, but is so huge and roomlessly undifferentiated inside that you can easily imagine it serving as a combination granary/conservatory for a rather large village or indeed small town. Polly peruses the aisles of dresses that greet her when they enter. Off one rack, she efficiently and without breaking stride swipes a blue thing that was probably once a bridesmaid dress or ironic prom dress, certain she can render it wearable with a simple ruffle-ectomy. Deeper within, Oliver scans the bookshelves without much optimism; as expected, most of the books thereon are either Stephen Kings (all of which he already owns) or bear the ovoid mark of Cain signalling their membership in Oprah's book club. Some sort of crockery-filled section is the final hurdle before they reach their ultimate destination, the area containing technology—defunct video game consoles (which Oliver also already has), Casio SK-1 keyboards piled upon each other, virtually daring you not to start humming the "demonstration" music. A drum kit (inferior to the one Polly, though a guitarist by nature, already has).

And: Oliver's guitar-to-be.

A red-bodied Les Paul knockoff that totally came from either Zellers or Canadian Tire originally and must have been donated to the VeeVee the moment the kid whose tenth-birthday present it was learned his fourth chord and upgraded to a real guitar. Its subtle curves like the figure of your dearest darling. It's even got a little kill switch to rapidly shift between a hot signal and complete silence, just like Tom Morello and Buckethead use, though this one is probably someone's DIY modification and not factory standard. Oliver goes straight for it, sweeps it up in his arms (it's sitting on a tiny amp that is included with the guitar!) and holds it to his face like he's listening for its heartbeat. And indeed, it feels a little warm, warmer than plasticized metal really ought to feel, and he can almost detect, he thinks, a slight, distant pulse emanating from inside it. It feels and sounds, comfortingly, like hugging his cat, except not furry and not trying desperately to escape from his needy clutches. Anyone who knew anything about guitars might have been slightly alarmed by these tonalities and temperatures. But not Oliver. No, Oliver is in love. He calls to Polly.

Polly sidles up, looks it over. "That guitar," she says, "is a complete piece of shit."

Oliver turns to her, grinning, holding the instrument to his face so it appears to sprout from the side of his head like a grotesque cybernetic tumour. Looking at Polly and the guitar at the same time makes Oliver so happy he could burst. "I know," he says. "Isn't it great?"

Polly's eyes narrow. Her gloved hands twist the blue dress between them. Her lips widen in something that's neither smile nor scowl. With total sincerity she says, "Yeah." She says, "It's pretty fucking great."

2006.
Tonight: The Oughts!

Behind the drum kit sits Polly. On the kick drum's front, she's drawn an angry face, a big circle with two little circles for eyes, down-slanting lines for eyebrows, and a jagged lightning-bolt type line for a mouth, in chisel-tip Sharpie. Inside the drum, she's stuffed a couple of sweatshirts. A microphone to her left, just behind the hi-hat, points at her mouth.

Up front stands Oliver, guitar slung diagonally, expertly lazy across his body, looking out at the crowd (such as it is), rising nervously up to toes and dropping back down to rubber soles. His guitar's amp cord snakes around behind him on the wooden stage floor of the Palace, the last sleazy club on the fastest-gentrifying street in the city, a club that looks and smells like the inside of a crate of whiskey and is about the same size.

Oliver turns to Polly and shrugs. Polly nods, pulls her drum gloves down over her wrists, gets a better grip on her drumsticks, knocks them together four times fast, and they're off.

Polly wrote this song. Polly writes all their songs. Oliver is fine with this because he couldn't write a song if John Lennon himself held a gun to his head. Not John Lennon's head. Oliver's head. Maybe that image is in bad taste. How about: He couldn't write a song if he found Bob Dylan's dream journal on a bus. Or some more contemporary reference. Jack White's family hymnal. James Murphy's ... flash drive? I don't know. The point is he's tried songwriting, and failed, every single time. It turns out, though, that what he can do is perfectly mimic the chords that Polly shows him and downtune when necessary. The Oughts are thankful that guitar solos are out of fashion. Oliver can also shout the last word of every line of Polly's lyrics while she sings and assaults the drums like they ran over her dog. You have never heard two people produce this much noise. When someone asks what The Oughts sound like, Polly says, "Like Elliott Smith joined Slayer," and then that person usually shuts up.

The Oughts have been playing for twenty minutes. No banter. They're the first of four bands playing at the Palace tonight. Hardly anyone is there —it's not even dark outside yet—but a fairly healthy mosh pit froths in front of the stage.

Minute twenty-one, Oliver plays four notes and then all sound ceases to issue from his terrible old red guitar. He looks down at it in disappointment but not surprise. Strum strum strum: nothing. He hasn't hit the kill switch. There should be sound. He clicks the thing a couple of times anyway, just to see what happens, but to no effect. Polly goes on for a few more seconds with her high-tempo four-fours, then, scowling, stops. She screams into her mic: "Thank you!" Someone in long hair and a white t-shirt slips on the floor at the abrupt finish, but he looks okay; someone else picks him up and receives a grateful high-five. Sparse applause bids them farewell. No "You Suck"s from the peanut gallery, which is actually kind of a big deal for The Oughts. Oliver and Polly disassemble their gear. Polly whispers into Oliver's ear, "For the love of fuck, if you don't get a new guitar, I will destroy you." Oliver really feels sort of bad about it. The switch inside of him, the crush switch, doesn't quite seem to be working correctly either.

2003.

White cotton bandages wrap thick around Polly's hands, except at the very ends of her fingers, where the cotton is a dread-dark red. Her sharp green eyes, too, are red. Oliver enters the room; when Polly looks up and sees him, she raises herself onto her elbows on her hospital bed nest.

"Hey," Oliver says.

"Hi," Polly says.

Her parents filled him in when he got here. All he knew was that she was suddenly taken from school by ambulance to the hospital. The rumours were gruesome. What everyone agreed: metal shop class, activated lathe, someone accidentally knocking her from behind, her hands going up in auto-defence, and then.

"How are you feeling?" Oliver asks.

"I'm on a lot of drugs, so the pain isn't so horrible," Polly says.

"That's good."

"And I guess I'll save a lot of money on nail polish from now on."

"Uh huh."

"But otherwise, pretty terrible."

"Yeah. I'm sorry."

"Thanks for coming," she says. She starts to cry again for the God-knows-how-manyth time today. She says, "My life is totally ruined."

Oliver moves to her bedside. The normal thing would be to comfort her by holding her hand, but you know.

"Your life isn't ruined," Oliver says. Trying really hard himself not to cry. Seeing her like this.

"Of course it is," Polly says. "I was going to be a musician; I was going to be in the best band in the world—that's all I ever wanted to do, ever. Now what? I'm fucked. I won't even be able to tie my shoes."

"You can still be a musician," Oliver says. "You can still be in the best band in the world."

"Don't give me that shit, Oliver," Polly says. She holds up her hands, mummified in cotton. "My motherfucking fingertips are gone! Up to the first fucking knuckle, Oliver. Do you understand? I can't play guitar like this! I'll never play guitar again." Hands drop hopeless to her lap. Dead orange hair sticks to her face in tense vertical strings where tears paste it fast.

"I'm telling you, you can do it," Oliver says. "I would not bullshit you; you know I wouldn't bullshit you." Polly sniffs and Oliver continues. "You can play drums," he says. "You already play drums. You can still sing. You can still write songs."

"It's not the same!" Polly says. "I can't play guitar! How can I write guitar songs if I can't play? The songs have to be mine, do you understand? There's so much music in my head. There's so much ... " She trails off into despair. Oliver swallows hard.

"I'll play for you," he says. "I'll play guitar."

"Oliver," Polly says, "you know I love you, but as a guitarist you suck."

This is where Oliver finds that crush switch inside him and clicks it off for the first time.

"I suck because I never cared enough to practise. I wouldn't even look at the sheets from one class to the next because I was too lazy. I don't have any music inside. But for you, I'll care. I'll buy a guitar, and I'll sit with you every day, and I'll play anything you tell me. I'll be serious. Okay? Because I love you too." Now's when he also starts to cry. "Okay?"

Twin shining trails race down both sides of Polly's face. She looks at Oliver, at his eyes. She smiles.

"What do you think," she says, "of The Oughts? For the name of our band. Like the decade. I've been saving it."

Oliver moves in, slides the hair away from Polly's face with his fingertips. He says, "It's perfect."

2009 again.
Sitting on his bed, Oliver clutches his guitar to his chest. "I'll get it fixed!" he says.

"Thank you," says Polly. Rises from her chair and makes for the door of Oliver's bedroom, wading through an ankle-deep slough of athletic socks. "Now I have to go, but remember you promised," she says. "Studio. Monday. Working guitar."

"I'm on it."

Polly smiles, which doesn't happen often, but is totally worth it when it does.

"You're a good one," she says.

Oliver smiles back at her. These moments, he thinks, this is why we're friends. What he loves is her honesty. Her honesty, her self-awareness. Those bursts of geniality taste extra sweet when they come from her. And her jawline. She's got a really exquisite jawline.

Polly wraps her gloved, truncated hand around the doorknob, turns it, and then she's out and Oliver is alone.

When he raises the guitar up to his ear, he thinks he can hear the ocean. A soft knock with knuckles on its body elicits a sort of echo from what sounds unaccountably deep inside.

"I can do this," he says aloud to himself. "Probably just one loose wire on the cable-input side." He says this out loud because he's proud to know a term like *cable input* even though there's no one around to hear it. But Polly would be impressed. Yes she would. He's never opened up his guitar before, but he's sure there's nothing to it. Faster and cheaper to do it himself. And way more punk. That sound like metal, like dirty, grinding feedback, rises higher.

Oliver takes the guitar to his desk and lays it down flat on its front. Rectangular hairline groove demarcates the instrument's removable panel, Phillips-head screws at every corner, allowing access to the main body cavity. Retrieves a screwdriver from a desk drawer and puts it to work, tip of his tongue peeking from between his lips in concentration. Top left. Top right. Bottom left. Bottom right. He lays the screws down carefully on the desktop, head-to-tail to prevent their rolling away. With surgical reverence, pulls away the panel.

Though only a couple of inches at its thickest, somehow the guitar's interior is at least a foot deep. Inside: no wires. Instead he's looking into the exposed chest cavity of a living being.

Oliver sees a pair of smoker's pink-grey lungs in there. Inflating, deflating. Breathing. Breathing slow, uneven. But breathing. And like a pair of fists fighting to escape a sewn-up pouch of muscle and gristle, a livid heart pumping. Diaphragm tense as a drum at chamber's floor, esophagus and trachea quivering vertical, bisecting the space. A transit map of veins and nerves and arteries.

And Oliver's like, what the fuck is this. Is he dreaming or drugged or dying or dead. Or what.

From around organs' edges now, dark, shining blood swells up and spills out over the guitar's hollow perimeter. Not pooling like water but beading like mercury, staining vermilion the wooden desktop. Heart pounds faster. Blood keeps flowing.

Oliver slams the panel down over the hole hard enough to knock the removed screws off the desk's surface. They hit the ground and jump apart and roll away and disappear. Oliver pulls up the carpet of socks and sweatshirts from the floor and piles them frantically atop the hemorrhaging guitar until it's gone. He doesn't care. He'll just have to ... something. And he'll never tell anyone about what happened here today, nobody, not ever.

Boring

"Don't cry. It's not punk. Sid Vicious got bored, not scared.
Drugs, radiation: dull as dust. Dying? I promise," he said,
"boringboringboring."

 **Baby**

FINALLY, FINALLY ASLEEP.

My turn, because it's Sunday, to get up whenever it does, so the wife can be relatively well-rested in the morning. We each get alternate days to be dangerously exhausted at work. Because we're a team, see.

A minute ago the thing in the crib was howling as if on fire—then suddenly laughing uncontrollably like the Marx Brothers just showed up at its birthday party. Now sleeping, bulbous little belly plumbobbing up and down with every breath.

On the wall above the crib, the big, blue cartoon lion stenciled there disapproves of me, mane a disconnected mess of green curls. Big ovoid eyes tilted inward in a strangely mournful expression, the lion says, *Some father you are.*

Yeah, well. Some lion you are. Go chase a zebra.

A weird combination of envy and pity bubbles up in me Alka-Seltzer style. Was I *ever* as happy as the thing in the crib seems to be when I stick my tongue out at it? And if that little pink blob thinks that five minutes alone in the dark warrants the doomsday-siren psychic breakdown I just witnessed ... well, hell, baby, you have no idea how bad it really gets.

You will.

Silently into the crib I say, *If I were a different kind of*, and I have to stop and start again because I can't use the word *man* even only in my own head, because what's a man? *If I were a different kind of person*, I say into the crib silently, *right now I'd be downstairs with one hand wrapped around a tumbler of scotch and the other holding a loaded handgun.*

No hard liquor permitted in the house. Makes the wife uncomfortable. Only white wine, which I do not care for. Her father is an alcoholic, see. First time the in-laws came over here, the day we brought the baby home from the hospital, the wife's father had a smile so wide it looked surgical. His big beard hanging off him like leaves on a dead willow tree, brown and serrate. When I don't shave for two weeks, the skin on my cheeks turns to ground veal with rusty nails sticking out. He slapped me on the back, and he said, "Let's celebrate with a drink!"

The wife said, "Dad, we don't keep liquor in the house." And I watched the guy just *deflate*. All of a sudden, he was one of those blow-up Bozo the Clown punching bags that got hit in the face fifty or a hundred times too many. He said, "Oh." Then the baby started to cry.

And it's a huge pain in the ass to obtain a firearm in this country besides. So instead, the father of the thing in the crib trundles downstairs for a cup of tea, the staircase a minefield, every creaking footstep swollen with threats of mortality, because I'm pretty convinced that if the thing in the crib wakes up again it's all over. Thank God, I make it to the kitchen. Fill the kettle with water as silently as possible, my face reflecting mutated in the stainless steel. Noise is my enemy. Electrical cord is a little bit wet from water that's leaked onto the counter, but I plug it in anyway and nothing harmful occurs—just the sound of softly blowing wind from inside the kettle that's water molecules accelerating.

Shortly after delivery, we went to the pediatrician. Same pediatrician that the wife saw when she was little. "I trust her more than anyone," is what the wife said. Pediatrician in her mid-sixties, short, hair naturally curled and naturally grey, deep, deep smile lines at her eyes like impressions of pitchforks. Asked, "Any depression?" Asked the mother, mind you. Nobody asks the father. Exam room's walls painted blue and dark as Lead Belly's soul. Art print hanging there of a toddler in an old-timey doctor's office, either lowering or replacing her pants, buttocks hanging out Coppertone-style, while she fastidiously scrutinizes the various diplomas and miscellaneous credentials posted around the room. The wife answered, "Nope! I feel great." Chirped it, really. Just shining, just genuinely radiating joy and love for her beautiful newborn child. Who, lying naked on the paper-covered exam table, as if on cue, suddenly shit the colour and texture of bananas, and the women laughed together. They went on to share a few amusing anecdotes about perineal lacerations.

This is life. This is what life is now.

Before the kettle starts to scream, I unplug it. Water sound never rises beyond a boiling breath. So easy. I pour into a white ceramic hemisphere with eyes closed, only to hear the lion, the stupid flat blue lion that's the only one watching the baby, say, *You forgot the teabag.*

So I did. The father of the thing in the crib says, *So I did. Okay. Nobody died.* And drops a teabag in, slowly dyeing the water to bile, and carries it back upstairs to the bedroom. Master bedroom.

Mother of the thing in the crib lying on her right side, spine curved, head bowed, legs and arms bent and drawn toward herself in a hug. I can only sleep on my left. Her eyes are moving and her lips smile, and from the other room the flat blue lion asks, *Do you think it's any easier for her?* Sarcasm. Because of course it's not. She is no less tired than I am, certainly no less a martyr. She was the one giving up her bodily integrity for upwards of a year while I stood by her feet doing nothing. I have not been granted permission to complain. If watching *her* become *them* kills my capacity to think of myself as anything but the father of the thing in the crib ever after, then that's just that. Happens to everybody. No other choice.

The tea is still too hot, and not yet tea. You take every drop of that parental leave because what the hell, the baby is the only reason you have this job anyway. Because money. Because insurance. Because two bedrooms, because backyard that needs weekly mowing eight months out of the year, because eavestroughs and car seats and private school. When God gives you the keys to the front door of your new fully detached suburban neo-eclectic, He also assiduously seals all the other exits. When we were scouring the baby-name books for something not too common but not too hipster, I turned straight to the *F*s. But *Failure* was not an option, see. The mother of the thing in the crib in the bed, smiling and dreaming and alive.

The teacup carries me back into the baby's room. In the crib, in the dark, it might as well be underwater.

Why did you do it, then? That's the flat blue lion again, while I stand over the crib with scowling mouth and scalding cup. *If it's such a horrible life, then why? Nobody forced you.* So here's why. We were meeting after work one day. The wife, before she was the wife. Our offices were only blocks away from each other, but she finished half an hour later than I did, so typically we'd meet at a coffee shop and sit. Before marriage, we did not live together. Traditional, see. Fifteen, maybe twenty minutes, I'd sit with coffee alone and wait for her.

One day, waiting there for her, she startled me. I shouldn't have been startled. I shouldn't have been startled because she didn't sneak up; she walked through the café door in full view and headed right for me. A beeline. A shark-line. I should not have been startled, but I was. I thought, who is this person and why are they coming to my table? Not until she was almost upon me did I realize. She sat down, lips full of incredulous giggles at my obvious, inexplicable shock. So I proposed. Not to shock her back. Though it did that. Though she said yes. Though I didn't have so much as a ring. No, I hadn't come down with an acute case of face-blindness. No aneurysm turning reckless my over-cautious brain. Not prosopagnosia but *macular degeneration*. Not until her face was at arms-length could I recognize her. My father, it struck me in that moment, started wearing glasses when he was the age I was then. I remembered it. The day he came home wearing glasses for the first time, I didn't recognize him, just like I didn't recognize her. I was young the day my father came home with his newly bordered face, but I was *alive*, I was conscious and capable of creating memories when my father was the same age I was sitting drinking coffee across a table from her.

That's why, you dumb lion, you arrogant flat blue cat. If you must know. It was time to give up, that's why. About the right time for the woman I loved to become the woman I'd fight with over the thermostat for the rest of our lives; for the woman I'd lusted after since the first time I saw her across a wall of dirty dishes at an even dirtier diner, since the first time I set eyes on her—back when eyes were eyes—time for her to become the weird screaming meat expelling smaller screaming meat. Whose breasts are *food*. Whose body is *Mommy*.

Time to admit defeat. To become the father of the thing in the crib. The blurry pink emblem of failure that means I'm happy if I can have five consecutive minutes of silence. Looking down, in the dark, without my glasses, I can just about almost not see it. Tea getting cold. I let it.

Poisoner

"YOU'RE GONNA HAVE SUCH A FANTASTIC LIFE, I SWEAR," ADAM says. He drains the tumbler of rum and Coke, his sixth, starts looking around for the bottles. "Just watch," he says, "you're gonna get on that plane tomorrow night; you're gonna get off in a whole new hemisphere. One year from today, you're gonna have your master's degree—" He finds the two litre Coke bottle, crushed into an unrecognizable modern-art spiral of plastic, about three hundred millilitres of cola remaining, under the pillow on which he's sitting. He slurs a smile, holds up the bottle and unscrews the top, pours the remaining liquid into the glass on the floor beside him. He says, "You'll be all full of brilliant new ideas, so full that you'll need to drag buckets behind you when you walk to catch any of them that might sweat out of you. You'll make a billion bucks, and you'll—where the fuck is the rum?"

I lean over and return the bottle of Bacardi Gold to him. Just wanted to see when he'd notice. He takes it from me, empties it into his glass. Swishes it around a bit. Doesn't drink it yet. He says, "You're gonna ... where was I?"

I remind him: "I'm a billionaire."

"Right! You're a billionaire, and you'll meet the girl of your dreams. Some hot little thing, with blond hair, natural, the way you like them, who reads, like, Proust or something. And not a skank, either. You'll get married and have a swarm of kids and live happily ever after."

"Thanks." I gulp the remains of my drink. My seventh, I think.

"You don't sound convinced."

I'm not convinced. Adam is the one with the good job. He's

the one getting married next year. He's the one engaged for five months to the hot young thing, Naomi, with her miles of dark brown ringlets and her eyes that are always scrunched up like she's trying to see something really far away. Adam and Naomi met at midnight on a beach six thousand miles away, on separate group tours, and discovered that he'd gone to high school with her older sister.

That kind of romantic shit never happens to me.

I say, "Adam, drink your drink."

He sips from his glass, puts it back down on the tile floor with a clink.

He closes his eyes, lays back, and says, "I'm really gonna miss you, man."

"I'll be back for the wedding," I say.

No response.

I recline in my leather beanbag and waste a dramatic, pathetic sigh. After a while, when I'm absolutely sure that he's asleep, I steal Adam's last rum and Coke and down it. It tastes absolutely evil, like some demon took a shit in the glass. I fight off the urge to vomit, and the urge to cry, and I fall asleep.

It's only when I wake up the next morning that I realize that at the point I took his drink, Adam had probably already been dead for about twenty minutes.

I'm the one who finds the body, of course, so I'm the one who calls 911. I'm the one who sits with him in the ambulance, even though he's been gone for hours, and I'm the first one to whom the doctor says, "I'm sorry." Even before Adam's parents, who I have to call. It's me, all me, all alone with this thing that used to be my best friend. All alone.

It was alcohol poisoning. Or maybe it was a massive spontaneous brain hemorrhage or a previously undetected congenital heart defect. Or a voodoo curse. They tell me, but somehow I don't hear. A lot of different people seem to be screaming at me all at once, most of them inside my head. When Naomi arrives at the hospital, I have to leave. I can't talk to her. I'll let his parents explain. I have to go.

As luck would have it, my flight is cancelled due to maintenance concerns, so I just reschedule and I can attend the funeral two days later, no problem.

At the funeral home, some rabbi speaks then Adam's father speaks, but I don't hear a single word. Adam's father's eyes are red as sunset, and he doesn't even bother hiding behind dark glasses. Adam's mother looks utterly hollow; I'm afraid a wind might come and blow her away any minute. Adam's sister looks like a shattered plexiglass window. I've known her since she was six.

At the cemetery in the afternoon, while I'm helping to shovel dirt onto Adam's coffin, I hear it for the first time. Suddenly all the screaming evaporates, and there's only a single voice left inside my head, and it tells me that Adam was the one who stole my Ninja Turtle action figure when we were ten. It's the stupidest thing, but all of a sudden I'm gripped with this certainty that he took Raphael when I wasn't looking and never gave him back. I never found it; I had to buy a new one. I don't know where this idea came from. I'd never suspected Adam of theft before, and I had no evidence. Just this voice whispering inside me. And that's not proof.

I do a lot of hugging and asking, "Are you okay?"

Adam's dad smells like Johnnie Walker and says, "I just can't believe it." His mom smells like salt and doesn't respond at all.

Naomi smells like shampoo and Marlboro Lights, and she says, she squeaks, "No." She presses her face into my chest, soaking a death mask into my shirt. I strangle a handful of her hair, and it spirals out on both sides of my fist. She says, "What's going on? Where am I?" and I can't tell if she's just in shock or if she's on drugs. She's still wearing the diamond engagement ring, I notice. And I have to suppress the desire to tell her what the voice inside my head is telling me right now: that Adam beat up the owner of a pawn shop to get that ring for her, even though I know for a fact that it isn't the least bit true.

The next day I get on a plane, and I watch the world turn to flashing Lego outside then disappear completely. I fly away across the ocean, and when the world comes back, I'm convinced that Adam had been blackmailing his boss for more than a year.

School starts off okay. I settle into my classes. I'm amused by people's accents. I do my assignments and get decent but not spectacular grades. Often I think of Adam's prophecy for my life from the night he died; I scrutinize every blond, non-skanky girl I see. Rarely do I say a word to any of them. Okay, never.

On weekends, I don't go out at night. Instead I sit in my absurdly tiny dorm room, stare at the ceiling, and listen to the voice in my head slander the hell out of my dead best friend. Adam was a serial cat killer. He would put out open cans of tuna to attract strays, and he'd lace the fish with rat poison. Sometimes he would break kittens' necks before the poison even had a chance to work. Then he'd cut them open and tie their intestines together, stretch them out and use them to make Satanic symbols on the kitchen floor. He'd videotape it and jerk off to it later.

But, I mean ... no, of course he didn't. How could I possibly even imagine such a thing?

I start skipping classes, finding I can't concentrate anyway. The voice keeps getting louder, and no matter how high I play my music, I can't drown it out. Now Adam raped and murdered a homeless teenage runaway: chased her into an alley behind a porn theatre, fucked her like her daddy did, and then tore out two-thirds of her hair and smashed her brains out against the cold, filthy brick wall.

Instead of sleeping, I drink. It doesn't help. I guess it never does, really, but in this case especially. I hear the voice: it's the roar of the ocean with my head inside a giant seashell. It's claws scraping around the walls of a room made of chalkboards.

Adam was Jack the Ripper. He was Charles Manson. My best friend Adam, he was flying those planes.

On the day when I finally just can't take it anymore, I pick up the phone. It's around noon here, God knows what time it is where Naomi is.

"Hello?" she croaks. She must have been sleeping. She couldn't possibly have been crying this whole time.

"It's me," I say, and then I tell her. I tell her everything, every horrible lie that's been pouring into my head since the day her beloved fiancé went and left us all for no fucking reason. I tell her that Adam had cheated on her constantly. He would pick up prostitutes, sometimes two or three at once, and would fuck them in front of Naomi's high school graduation photo. He emptied condoms into her salad dressing. He pissed in her shampoo; he recorded her orgasms and played them for strangers in pubs. He fucked all her friends. He fucked both her sisters. At the same time. Even Jill, the ten-year-old.

The bile, the lies, spewing out of my mouth and across the world, and it's all that demon-shit taste of the last drink that Adam ever poured.

Naomi is hysterical, in tears.

"Why are you saying those things?" she shrieks at me. "You know it's not true! You were his best friend! Are you crazy? What's wrong with you?"

And I just have no idea. Honestly, I wish I knew. Something wants Adam's good name blotted out; something wants his life destroyed.

But his life *is* destroyed. Something took care of that already. So what do I think I'm doing?

Halfway across the planet from my best friend's rotting corpse and his grieving loved ones, I hang up the phone.

A Citizen of Terror

EVERYONE SAYS THE NEIGHBOURHOOD IS CHANGING. PEOPLE WHO LIKE what's going on, they call it renewal. The rest call it gentrification. Mikey, though? Doesn't care. His dad owns the building they live in, so if he gets to raise the rent and the sketch-ass Sri Lankan grocery store has to move out and something better moves in instead, like a high-class massage parlour or whatever, all the better. Maybe that would clear out the junkies clustering around out front at night like the cockroaches that cluster inside, using the pay phone and breaking the windows once a month. The junkies, not the cockroaches. Not that it matters either way to Mikey. His dad's voice echoes in his mind, saying, *There's nothing to be afraid of*. So Mikey tells himself: there's nothing to be afraid of. He thinks: I'm not afraid of those punk-ass crackheads. I'm not afraid of anything.

Mikey's dad doesn't ever get home until late, late, late, so after school lets out Mikey's pretty much on his own. One time, his friend Marty's brother was going to play chicken with some other guy out behind the high school on that concrete strip that isn't even a street, so Mikey and practically everyone else went to watch. Marty's brother in his new blue Civic (well, used Civic, but he'd only had it a couple of weeks, so it was new to him) and the other guy at the other end of the strip in his mom's VW station wagon, which Mikey and his crew thought was the stupidest thing they'd ever seen. About a million people all on the sidelines watching, but they were kids, mostly from the high school, but some, like Mikey and his friends, younger. No adults of any kind. Literally, Mikey could have looked up and seen into the window of the science lab from where he stood, it was only like twenty metres from the soccer field, but the teachers and whoever must have been idiots or didn't care or both. The principal ended up getting fired afterwards, though.

So the cars revved up, and you wouldn't have thought a stupid beige station wagon's engine could make that much noise, but it did, so evidently you never know. Somebody in the middle of the strip held his arm up and counted to three and lowered his arm, and the cars just tore off at each other at top speed, and you could hear the tires shrieking even over the screams of the kids cheering them on. And the fun part obviously was which one of them is going to pussy out, right?

Mikey didn't have the best view, but what happened was that when the cars were about two seconds away from colliding, Marty's brother pussied out and swerved off to the right. Except the guy with his mom's station wagon at the exact same time also pussied out, and he swerved in the same direction, the wagon's left, which was the Civic's right, and the two of them ended up crashing anyway.

Nobody died or anything like that, but Marty's brother broke both his arms and collarbone in about fifteen places each. The other guy lost most of his vision. Mikey heard he still gets headaches too, that kid. Blood all over the place, like the time when Mikey caught a mosquito on his arm mid-bite, and while it was still sucking on him, he grabbed the skin around it and squeezed. That's what the front seat of the wagon looked like. Head wounds bleed *a lot*. Both the kids got expelled from school, and one girl who was just standing there watching almost got her leg amputated when a hubcap came flying off and practically cut through her knee like a buzzsaw. Like *rrrryyyyoooowwww*. Some dirt got in Mikey's mouth.

The whole thing was such a big deal at the time that the cops even came to *his* school—where no one was old enough to drive yet, not even the kid who got left back—to tell them how stupid those kids were and how you got to have some common sense and behave sensibly behind the wheel. And don't drink and drive, which no one was even doing anyway, so. Mikey thinks that's all crap though. To him the moral of the story is pretty obviously *don't pussy out*.

If you walk about twenty minutes from Mikey's place, you get to the train tracks. There's no station there; it's just the tracks, and it's practically the middle of nowhere, considering how close it is to Mikey's place and the school. Abandoned industrial buildings on one side and just a field full of overgrown nothing on the other side. Scariest thing Mikey and his friends ever found exploring those old industrial buildings was a huge dead raccoon, even that wasn't really scary at all if you ask him, and everyone else is just a pussy.

Sometimes they jump over the tracks. They go and jump over the tracks, over and over, back and forth until the train comes, seeing how many times they can jump. You get more points the later you jump, but the points don't mean anything. It's just to see who's afraid of getting run over and who isn't. Mikey is not. Marty didn't used to be, but ever since the thing with his brother, he'll barely jump anymore at all. Mikey looks at him standing there and not jumping and thinks Marty has like no balls now, none; his mom controls his whole life and blames herself for what happened to his brother, and so now she has to know what everyone is doing every single second of every day. Mikey doesn't like going to Marty's house anymore. Everyone else is somewhere in the middle. Funny thing, if you ask Mikey, is none of them ever got hit by that train. The one time anyone got actually hurt was when Jim's shoelace got caught on the rail during a jump, and he fell and twisted his ankle and scraped up his face pretty bad. Train didn't come for another half hour after that. Which to Mikey's mind, pretty much proves that if you don't pussy out, you're gonna be fine, and there's no point being afraid. When the train does come, it's pulling so many cars full of who-the-hell-knows-what that it takes like half an hour to pass by, and you get bored throwing rocks and pop cans and whatever at it and go home.

So after school they're walking, throwing stuff at other stuff, when the sky gets all dark, closes in, and dumps about a swimming-pool-per-second of rain all over them out of nowhere. And it's *sharp*, the drops actually *hurt*, and they're wearing short sleeves because it's still not so cold yet, and it's like someone's pounding nails into Mikey's arms, and when he gets home are his arms gonna look like those junkies' or what? Marty and Jim make a run for it to who knows where. But they're just down the street from Mikey's place anyway, so he figures why speed up? You're already wet. You're just gonna run into the same amount of rain anyway and look like a spaz. And maybe even slip and crack your skull open on the sidewalk and spill your brains all out for dogs and raccoons to eat. Like, it's only water. What are you, made of sugar? Relax. He's ready to shout this at them, but he doesn't know where they went, Marty and Jim, after they started running, and when he gets to his building, they're not anywhere around, so he thinks, screw those guys anyway. Those pussies.

The building is a hundred this year, one hundred actual years old. And so is the lady who lives on the third floor, as far as Mikey can tell. They live in the apartment on the second floor, he and his dad, above the sketch-ass Sri Lankan grocery store, which is totally sketch-ass but has some really hilarious off-brand products and the *bibikkan* is pretty good so whatever. There's no air conditioning in the summer, and the heat tends to crap out in the winter, and the water pressure is pretty bad, but that doesn't bother him too much. Mikey's not really there much either. What's left of the building's original plumbing is lead. What's left of the original wiring is aluminum. Mikey knows this because of how much his dad complains about how expensive it is to replace that shit every time part of it stops working. What's left of the original occupants is nothing.

Going up the narrow stairs after fumbling with his key in the off-to-the-side entrance, he's dripping all over, and his shoes slip a couple of times, but he doesn't fall down and kill himself or anything like that. But he remembers that wooden marionette he had when he was little, the time he dropped it down this staircase—an image flashes in his mind of his own broken, bloody body at the bottom of the stairs, just like that wooden marionette, leaning up against the inside of the door, ready to just spill out like a bag of laundry the next time someone opens it, scaring the shit out of them. This seems pretty funny for a few seconds until suddenly it doesn't anymore.

The staircase is tight and steep and white drywall with one sixty-watt bulb hanging from the ceiling. Climbing the stairs feels like they turned the gravity up two or three times normal. It opens into a sort of landing, and then you have to turn around and go up another flight of stairs to get to the apartment and then another one if you want to go up to the third floor. The two apartments used to be just one, way back before his dad even bought the building, and so they still share a single bathroom, which is on the landing between the staircases and inconvenient to a retarded degree and right now locked, which means the old lady from the third floor is in there probably taking a bath. She's nice and everything, always been friendly to Mikey, and she's clean and quiet, and his dad says she always pays her rent on time, and Mikey doesn't have a problem with her as a person, but her baths take goddamn forever. Her kids and grandkids moved back to either Barbados or Trinidad, she told Mikey once, but he doesn't remember which one now. That was like twenty-five years ago that they moved, so Mikey never met them, but the old lady has lived all alone up there since then, and she can't take showers because of the water pressure, and also she can't stand up for very long, and sometimes if she's in there for a really long time, Mikey's dad'll knock to make sure she's still alive. Mikey thinks his dad actually believes she's going to die in there one day. She is pretty old, and she's all alone here, and if she dies Mikey's dad'll have to call up her family and tell them because there's no one else to do it, and that's not exactly going to be a whole lot of fun for him. Mikey imagines her all naked and pruney and swollen up dead underwater in the tub. There's no way in torrential hell he's going to knock on that door. But he thinks he can hear some splashing in there. So she's probably okay. He runs up to the apartment and to his room and strips off his wet clothes and throws them on the floor and puts on some dry ones after towelling off.

His dad's not home, of course. Sometimes Mikey wonders why they have to live in the worst one of the buildings his dad owns. Sentimental reasons, he guesses. Like he doesn't want to sell it, but it would cost more than it's worth to gut the place and fix it up. Now that the neighbourhood is getting all trendy, maybe the property value will go up enough to make selling it worth it, and they can go somewhere else. Not that Mikey hates it here. It's fine. School is close and all his friends. He just wishes there was, for instance, a bathroom *inside* the actual apartment. Also if his dad sold the building or even gutted it and fixed it up, he'd have to throw the old lady from the third floor out on the street. Probably he doesn't want to do that either. Good tenants like her are hard to find, he says. You have to really take care of the good ones. So maybe he's just waiting for her to die. So yeah: sentimental reasons.

But right now, Mikey's really gotta take a piss. And who knows

how long she's gonna be in there. Mikey's too old to be peeing in
mason jars anymore when the bathroom door is locked. He peed out
the window once. That was funny. There *is* another bathroom, if you
can call it that, but it's all the way down in the basement.

He puts his shoes back on then goes out to the hallway, down to
the first floor, and then down the next set of stairs to the basement.
Flick the switch at the top, and the only light is from another naked
bulb hanging down, this one only thirty watts and grimy and caked
with clotted bug crap. No one comes down here unless the heat goes
out or a fuse blows. A *fuse*, that's how old this building is—not even *if
the breaker trips* but *if a fuse blows*. It's unfinished, the walls and the
ceiling grey bricks that look like they could just be the settled dust of
a century of abandonment. At the bottom of the stairs, the floor lies
uneven, sinks down into a pit more than a foot deep in the middle,
and tiles cracked into a spiderweb pattern span almost the whole
room. Mikey envisions someone in the twenties coming down here,
dropping a cannonball or something and breaking the foundation.
Sound of dumbass insects, woken up by the light, knocking themselves
into the bulb over and over and over, like someone tapping fingernails
on your bedroom window in the middle of the night, click crack
crunch. They never learn, so it never stops, so that's the soundtrack
of this basement, and it makes it feel a lot like a horror movie in here.
But Mikey likes horror movies. He thinks they're funny. So that's okay.

The bathroom is about the size of Mikey's locker at school but
with a toilet in it instead of a Led Zeppelin poster. But he only needs
to take a piss—he's not having a birthday party in there or anything,
so it's fine. When he's done, he goes back out, and there's still the
sound of those bugs just bashing their brains out up there. Mikey
hasn't been to the basement for a couple of years, maybe more. He
can't really remember when. So he decides to look around a little.

It doesn't take long. The place is not large. Furnace inside a sort
of alcove. Thick, green dinosaur-vein wires affixed to the walls. Pipes
wide as Mikey's arms running along the ceiling, water shaking out
a metallic whine from inside them. What's behind the furnace? He's
never looked. Explored everything around here for miles but not his
own basement. That's ridiculous, he thinks.

Furnace not actually right up against the wall but a couple of feet from the corner of the alcove and maybe six inches out. But when Mikey really gets in there to look closer, he notices it's not even a wall behind it. Just a big wooden board covering up a great big hole in the real wall. He can't push the board aside but can tilt it diagonally a bit. Back there he finds a black void, into which sight can't penetrate at all. So of course he has to go in. He can slide the board around enough so that a triangle of space opens up to let him and some light in. Gets down on the floor and imagines he must look like a goddamn chimney sweep from the accumulated filth. But it's going to be worth it. Mikey can still hear those bugs flying into the bulb, those little suicidal idiots. Click crack crunch. He crawls inside.

Even with the light from outside, it's not enough; he can't see a thing. On all fours, he moves forward a little farther. But there's nothing. Just the dust on the floor, on his clothes, in his lungs. Hard to tell how far he's gone with the small amount of light coming in behind him, but it seems to him like far. Dragging himself along, he wonders what this passage is for; does it go all the way to the end of the property or out even farther, maybe to the sewers? As soon as he decides to leave and come back with a flashlight and maybe a dust mask, he hears a soft sliding sound and then a loud *slam*, the wood plank falling back in place, and then suddenly it's absolutely perfectly dark instead of just totally dark, as the hole that goes back out to the basement closes.

He turns around, shuffling doglike, but then it occurs to him that he doesn't even know if he needs to stay down this way. Just because the hole was only this high, he figures, doesn't mean the space is. He reaches up and his hand touches nothing. Gets slowly to his knees. Still nothing. Rises up to his feet and still nothing. Reaches up with his arms over his head now and still nothing. So this room, space, whatever it is, is at least as tall as a regular-sized doorframe, which Mikey can touch the top of if he stands on his toes.

Darkness everywhere and everything. Mikey's brain hates this and starts showing him flashes of light and weird blobules of colours and shapes that float around in front of him like ghosts. There can only be, he estimates, at most a couple of metres between him and the wall, but it looks as if the darkness extends out, if not forever, then for hundreds of miles. Imagine you're standing at the top of a mountain or a really tall building and looking out, except there's nothing out there. Growing harder for him to breathe in here because of all the dust, and he closes his eyes because dust is getting into them too. But it doesn't help. Jim, with his asthma, would probably already be dead if he'd come in here.

Shuffles forward, toward the entrance. Slowly, because the last thing he wants is to trip and fall. Does he hear something? He thinks he does, something like whiny violins, which is maybe the pipes and maybe his ears doing the same thing that his eyes are doing, filling in the darkness, unknownness, the nothingness with somethingness because they don't know what else to do. Still moving forward. Pretty sure he should have hit the wall by now, where he should be able to find that plank and slide it or maybe kick it out of the way. But he hasn't yet. Maybe he got turned around? He really doesn't know for sure what direction he's going. Taking bigger steps now, and he's definitely gone at least as far as the entire length of the building and still no wall, no nothing. Walking at a normal pace now like he'd walk home from school, and he's just going farther and farther.

Stop.

This is dumb. Must be going in the wrong direction. Turns around again and starts going back this time. Keep going. Going going going. A full minute, then another. Nothing.

Something like lightning and something like a tangle of capillaries flares right in front of his eyes for a moment but actually doesn't. Keeps walking a dozen more seconds. A pinkish blob like a helium balloon full of cancer bobs into his field of vision, and he swipes at it with his hand, which he also of course can't see, and the blob disappears. But does he feel something like a cold wet tingle in his fingers when they slash through the shape that isn't there? No way. Another thirty seconds. Another wrong direction. Another endless dead end.

Stop again.

Long, thick, squamous things, gunmetal grey and with too many legs, eight or ten on each side, scrabble around at his ankles except not really. Their stone and metal feet, rounded and clawed toes, hundreds of them it sounds like, thousands, go click crack crunch across the floor, but no they don't.

Keep going, start again. This time, he resolves, he will walk and continue walking until he hits something, until he reaches a wall or a panel or, who knows, until a force field or a big, glowing stereoscopic splotch that doesn't exist forces him to stop.

Mikey tells himself: It can't just go on and on and on forever. It can't. Nothing goes on forever. Inwardly chants: There's nothing to be afraid of. His father's voice. There's nothing to be afraid of. Nothing, nothing, nothing.

Body Horror

IN THE MORNING THE ANTS ARE STILL THERE.

Their tiny, shiny feet scrabble across the floor, the grime in the grout betraying the minty medical green of the tiles. The ants are the colour of honey. Translucent like honey, too. They emerge, as always, from somewhere under the bed, streaming out, searching. Bedsheets same green as the floor, the walls, the ceiling. The gown The Boy wears lying on his stomach on the bed, half his face embedded in the pillow, one eye open and staring down, watching the workers leave for work.

There's not a lot to do here. The ants, they're always busy. The Boy has to make his own entertainment. He sleeps a lot. There's no cable. His dad never comes to visit. The medical staff all maintain their professional distance. In terms of social interaction, almost no one else in the ward is hinged enough to be interesting. He used to spend a lot of time complaining about the ant problem, until the men in charge stopped even pretending to care. Then he spent a lot of time in the so-called library—really it's just the room full of books that the families of patients couldn't get rid of because even used bookstores didn't want them; not like they're Dewey-ized or even alphabetical. At first he wanted to find some specific communicable disease carried by ants that he could bring to the attention of the doctors. So he scoured the reference texts for information about ants. What ended up happening instead is that he learned so much he stopped feeling afraid of them anymore. Now he likes the ants and is fascinated by them. Now he spends a lot of time watching them, thinking about them, imagining what it's like. What it's like to be an ant.

The Boy's body is squat and thick, the way it's always been. When

The Woman walks into the ward for the first time, The Boy doesn't know what to think. She is definitely over thirty. Her hair is cut short, a man's haircut. Her gown is loose, even for a gown, her breasts just shapeless masses under the green cotton. Her legs are too long. Her body makes no sense to The Boy. She makes no sense to him. The way she holds herself, the small steps, toes pointed in, her long-lashed eyes magnetized to the floor, making it clear that she makes no sense to herself either, that to be inside her is to be the punchline of a sadistic slapstick comedy routine.

The first time they speak is in the cafeteria at lunch. His orange plastic tray is piled with meat-sort-of-flavoured stuff the same colour and texture that his stool has taken on since his dad first checked him in. She is carefully adding salad leaves to hers that look less appetizing than the crab grass growing out front of the building. He asks her how many chromosomes she has, because what the hell are you supposed to say to a Woman. A Woman twice your age. She says, Forty-six, forty-six chromosomes, and he says congratulations, tells her that they are probably the only two people in this place that have the right number who don't get paid to be here. Ants, he says, most ants only have two chromosomes. *Two.*

Wow, The Woman says. That's not very many. The Boy agrees.

They go sit down at a table. A couple of nurses watch them.

Ants are haplodiploid, The Boy says. It takes him a while to say it. That means that the egg develops into a female if it gets fertilized, and if not then it becomes a male. And when they hatch and grow up, they just stay like that. For their whole life.

That's interesting, The Woman says. But I don't know if it sounds more complicated than necessary, or a lot less complicated than it ought to be. The Boy says yes, he doesn't know either.

How do you know so much about ants, The Woman asks.

The Boy says, Because there are ants in my room. They have a nest or something in a crack in the wall next to my bed. I can't get rid of them, so I found a book about them in the library here, and now I like them because I know everything about them.

I like cats, The Woman says. How many chromosomes does a cat have?

The Boy says he doesn't know. She asks him, Doesn't the library have any books about cats? And he says he doesn't know; he never looked for any books about cats, but maybe. The Woman suggests they go try to find one, so they finish eating their lunch, and then they go.

In the library, there is more dust than there are books, by volume, but there are still a lot of books, even if almost none of them have all their pages, were printed in the last fifty years, or have even a shred of anything worth reading inside them. The Boy usually has to content himself with books that fit only one or two of the above criteria at any one time. A lot of old *Reader's Digest* condensed novels and things like that with very strange stains or faint streaks throughout the pages. The Boy used to guess that they were printer's errors, but he knows now what they really are, because the book about ants has grown full of them since he arrived. Tears. Dried tears.

Nobody is in the library, because nobody is ever in the library, because there is no reason to be in the library unless you want a book or are hiding from someone or trying to commit suicide by provoking a fatal asthma attack. The staff can buy their own books elsewhere. The patients, even the few who haven't got most of their brain missing, their fingers don't work or their eyes are too far apart to be able to read properly anyway. Hiding is stressful if you can't turn your head to look for someone coming up behind you, which you can't do with a webbed neck or whatever you've probably got, which rules out the majority of the remaining patients. And the other thing, the last thing, there are easier ways to do that. Chances are if you're here, your heart or else your lungs are so stunted that you could end yourself just by double-timing it down the hallway, if you wanted to. So The Boy and The Woman are alone.

One by one, they sort through the books, the two of them do. All out of order.

Someone should organize these properly, The Woman says. One of these days.

The Boy agrees. He agrees with her a lot.

You were born like this, she says. Not a question.

He says yeah. And ... you?

I was born like this too. She laughs a little. Her long, thin fingers twist their way through her hair, but don't stop when they reach the bottom, like they've forgotten that it's short now. She must have cut it not very long ago. Still holding on. Her fingernails look cared for. She says, Things were pretty normal growing up. It was only in the last couple of years ... the last few years ...

Hey, The Boy says. Hey, this book. Look. Look what I found.

He holds out *The Cat Fanciers' Association Cat Encyclopedia*. Dressed in dust.

So she leans over and kisses him. And that's how it happens the first time. That's how it starts.

Later they learn that cats have thirty-eight chromosomes.

The medical staff does not like the two of them to spend time together. So it mostly happens at night. Mostly now he divides his life into equal parts sleeping, watching the ants, and spending time with her. Sometimes these overlap. They're almost impossible to get rid of, these ants. That's what The Boy learns. They're notorious for infesting hospitals, and they can nest anywhere, even between two sheets of paper. They get into electrical equipment and wreck it; they get into your open wounds and spread infection. When The Boy relates this last fact to one of the doctors, the doctor tells The Boy that he had better try not to get any open wounds, then. If you crush an ant, its body releases a chemical that other ants can smell, and they will freak out and attack.

You might be normal, The Woman tells him once. They're sitting on his bed. Watching the ants. Bare feet hanging down, knees bent, heels resting atop the side rails. Her bald calf against his newly bristly one. Gowns and bedsheets still the same minty medical green as ever. More like the colour of mint-flavoured chewing gum than actual mint leaves really. She looks at him and she says, In a few years, when you grow up some more, you'll be normal and then everything will be fine. You can get out of here. You can have a job and buy a house and get married and have a pile of kids of your own and all that stuff, and no one will ever have to know about what you were like before. What it was like. The Boy says, You could be normal too. You could wake up and be normal any day now. Next week. Tomorrow. Next time you check yourself out in the mirror, everything might be different. Just like that. The liquid look in The Woman's minty green eyes tells The Boy that it's something she really used to believe. When they both look back down to the floor, the ants are still there, running, running. Twitching full with pheromones and electricity. The ants are always there, always moving, always on their way somewhere. Always with somewhere to go.

What does this mean, The Boy asks one night, after.
    The Woman smiles at him kindly. What does what mean.
    This, he says. What does this mean.
    Shh. Shh, she says, holding his head gently in the crook of her arm. It's okay.
    What. I don't know what any of this means.

They organize the library first into fiction and non-fiction, then alphabetically by author, then chronologically by date of publication. They dust the books with baby wipes. When they're almost done with fiction, when they've just finished the authors whose surnames begin with *W*, that's when The Boy's father comes to get him. This is a month, maybe seven weeks, after The Woman arrived. It's hard to keep track in a place where nothing changes. Anyway, it's the day after someone vomited red and black and viscid on the floor of the TV room during an old episode of *The Twilight Zone*. Everyone knows, of course. About them. Everyone who is capable of knowing anything. In a place like this, secrets just don't keep. Someone tells someone else, and somehow things get out. The people can't get out, but the things do. It is not okay for two patients to behave this way. Completely inappropriate. The attorney-in-fact must be informed, particularly in a case involving a minor. Such as this.
    The staff members are uncomfortable with physical contact, so they only stand and watch as the father grabs The Boy to take him home. One imagines that there was an incident in the past that makes them reluctant to become personally involved. One imagines what they're like when they go home to their ... *whoevers*. Regardless, the junior nurses and medical interns play nervously with their hair or cross their arms across their breasts like links of chain mail. The RNs and senior physicians take up as much space as they can, widening their stances, stroking their beards. Pretending not to watch. Trying not to sneer.

The Boy's father dragging him out of the library, the big man's thick arms bent at the elbows like an ant's antennae, under his child's armpits, literally pulling his body away from this ... this *Woman*. She stands at the door to the library and watches, but doesn't say anything.

The Boy screams. Put me down. Leave me alone.

His father tells him that it's okay, that he's taking him somewhere else. Somewhere better. This place is no good for you anyway. The walls are cracked. There are ants all over the floor. The food is disgusting, and the people are creepy.

You don't understand. We're not done yet. We have to. We have to finish. We're only up to *W*. There's still letters left. There's still.

His father doesn't understand. Doesn't care to. Doesn't let go.

The Boy shouts back to the library: *X, X! X, Y!*

The Woman smiles, a little.

To his father, now, The Boy says, The ants all over the floor. Ants are haplodiploid. The queen lays eggs, like a million of them, and if an egg gets fertilized, the ant that hatches out is female, and if it doesn't get fertilized, then the ant that hatches out is male, and they stay like that, *they stay the same*. For their whole life. They stay the same. *It's normal.* It's normal.

once in the belly, then once down through his foot, nailing it fast to the hardwood floor. Literally nailed it, as in with a nail. They were building a bookshelf at the time. They argued. She flipped. She was off her meds. Well, they both were. See, they met in group therapy. He was new; she'd been going for a while already. She said, Hi, I'm Jane.

He said, Hi, I'm Henry.

Then she asked, So are you a drug addict or are you crazy? If you're here, you must be either crazy or a drug addict. Sort of an icebreaker.

Crazy, I guess, he said.

Good, she said. It's easier to get uncrazy than it is to get unaddicted. If you're a drug addict, you have to stop taking drugs, and that's hard, but if you're crazy, you just have to start taking drugs, and that's easy.

Henry couldn't really find a way to argue with that logic. They ended up going out for drinks after the therapy session, which was okay because neither of them were alcoholics, then going out for dinner, hanging out after work, and next thing they knew, they were dating, then they were in love, then they were moving in together, and then they were assembling a bookshelf.

Some days earlier they talked and mutually decided that they should try going off the meds for a while. The side effects were becoming unbearable: affecting their sleep, affecting their orgasms. They felt distant, from each other, from the world. Before, when they were still crazy, they didn't have each other. Now they did. Maybe that was what had been missing. Maybe they didn't even need the drugs anymore. How would they know if they didn't try? What do you think?

Waved bye-bye to the Seroquel then *vaya con Dios,* cold turkey. Which, yes, contraindicated. If you're going to go off, you're supposed to taper. But they were confident they wouldn't experience withdrawal; they had, after all, each other to draw into instead.

Building a new bookshelf became a necessity upon their cohabitation since they planned to merge their libraries into one. Everything all smiles and happy at first. Innocently, Henry mentions, between hammer blows, that when they first met, he didn't know why she was talking to him: if she actually found him attractive and interesting or if she just didn't know yet that he had no money and couldn't help advance her career, or what. Which profoundly offends her, which baffles and infuriates him, who shouts something unflattering, which makes her cry, which makes *him* cry, which makes her panic, which makes him freak out and strike the wall of the half-a-bookshelf with the hammer he's still holding, which makes her back up two steps, look at him with eyes telescopic wide—pupils cruising left to right as if reading the air above his head—and then pick a five-inch nail up off the table and pounce predatory, puncturing him through his Elliott Smith t-shirt just above the navel. Next comes the withdrawal: Jane pulls the nail from Henry, and he drops the hammer to plug the hole in his gut with both hands, staunch the blood spilling out like a can full of gasoline shot through with an arrow. Jane then nails his foot to the floor with her bare hands like she's planting her standard, metal through canvas, flesh, bone, rubber, and finally wood, leaving Henry screaming obscenities and standing in a growing blob of shadow the colour of cranberries. Jane runs and locks herself in the bedroom. Henry manages to reach the phone and call 911.

The foot required bandages and a tetanus shot. But the nail had actually perforated his stomach, and while he managed to keep from dying of blood loss, his stomach had spilt its contents into the abdominal cavity, and he almost ended up dying anyway of sepsis. She was charged with attempted murder. Pleaded insanity and got it because, after all, she was insane. They both were.

Two years later, she's released from the mental health centre. He comes to meet her. Back on the drugs and feeling fine. Both of them.

She says, You know, I never said I was sorry. Which I am. Sorry. But you don't know what it was like. You don't know what I saw. I was hallucinating. It was the scariest moment of my life. I saw you standing there holding the hammer, and then above your head, just floating there written in the air, I saw these bright red letters, glowing like the title of a horror movie, and they said: **HE IS GOING TO KILL YOU.** So that's why I did it. I was crazy, but I thought I was defending myself. I thought you were going to kill me. And he thinks for a second whether to say it or not to say it, but in the end he decides to say it. And he says, But I was. I was going to kill you. I really was.

 **?**

You were the first, that's why.

Wrong Side of Heaven

If you revisit the scenes of your happiness, your heart must burst of its agony.
—Dorothy Parker

DEAR EARTH,

You're 384,403 kilometres away, but it still seems like I could reach out and grab you. Since I'm in synchronous rotation around you, you're always visible up there in the sky. You wobble a little but never actually set, so I can look up and see you whenever I want.

How are you feeling? You're looking good. You're looking pretty.

Shine a light out your window at night, and it takes about a second and a half to reach me here. Our exploration vehicle took four days. It will take that same 1.5-ish seconds for this message to reach you when I press *send*. I don't know exactly when I'm coming back. I'm not totally sure that I am coming back.

Because our station is atop the rim of this crater at the north pole—since that's where the water is—it's permanent daytime here. The sky's always black because there's no atmosphere, but the station lives in a peak of eternal light. We have to sleep in rooms without windows. Or at least I do.

Where I'm sitting writing this, I like to call it *the garden*. That drives the actual astronauts crazy because it's more like a farm or a greenhouse, and a couple of them just call it by its module number (one zero zero one). But they're engineers and scientists. Technical types. Even the people who work here in the garden are botanists and entomologists. I'm the only liberal arts grad in the whole place. How about that: December Tenth, MFA—first civilian woman on the moon. Anyway, it reminds me of the garden behind Jamie Oakener's mum's house, with the kale and the tomatoes and the turnips and everything … and the bees, always with the bees. So I call it the garden, even though really it isn't.

What Jamie's mum's garden didn't have that this one does is the continual vacuum cleaner sound of the atmosphere generators and the endless grey expanse of completely desolate wasteland just on the other side of the fence.

Just like at Jamie's mum's, I like to sit here and drink coffee and write. Not the good coffee that Jamie would make us in the morning. Terrible coffee, thin, instant coffee, but coffee. Here I am, sitting, drinking coffee on the moon. That still gets me. I miss orange juice—the powdered crap that passes for orange juice around here tastes more like coffee than the coffee does—but the orange grove won't be harvestable for years yet.

An acute, whispery voice comes from behind me saying, "Don't move. Don't freak out, but there's a bee on you."

Always with the bees.

With a complaisant wave, Dr. Keats shoos away the bee from my shoulder. It alights and lands again on a nearby cucumber vine. Smiling, I turn to Dr. Keats as he stands beside me at the edge of the garden, the transparent barrier that encloses the station just inches in front of us.

I say, "Thanks, Jon."

The "there's a bee on you" thing is somewhere between an inside joke and a religious ritual at this point. Since I spend so much time in the garden, and since Dr. Keats is the head apiologist on the station, we see each other fairly often, and there is usually a bee on at least one of us. The fat, fuzzy bumblebees used here for pollination in the garden are really chill and non-aggressive, but you still need to take an allergy test before leaving Earth to make sure you won't die of anaphylactic shock, just in case you do something stupid and get yourself stung.

"Good morning, December," Dr. Keats says. "How are you doing?"

"Pretty good," I say. "Working on my post to send back to Earth." I gesture toward the blue globe in the black sky, as if I'm concerned he won't know what planet I mean.

"Cool," Dr. Keats says.

He's a small, grey, friendly man from California. Most of the station's occupants are American. Some are Canadian, like me, and there's also a handful of Russians. Some people from India, some from England. Ireland, Israel. Everyone gets along except during the World Cup.

He says, "Well, don't let me disturb you."

"Please," I say, grabbing the cuff of his white button-down—some people here wear their filmy aluminum-cotton space suits at practically all times, but Dr. Keats, like me, prefers casual dress even when he's on duty. I say, "Disturb me." I pull him down, and he sits beside me on the bench that's like a metal grate bent into a pair of right angles. Does that image even make sense?

"Having trouble writing?" Dr. Keats asks me.

I nod. "I don't think it's going to turn out very well. What am I doing here, Jon? I'm just some girl with a creative writing degree and one shitty novel. What was I thinking?"

Dr. Keats hasn't shaved for a few days; white coruscations of hair sit in the pores of his cheeks. "You're thirty years old," he says, smiling. "You're hardly a *girl*. And I'm certain that you wouldn't have been selected if you weren't up to the task."

He's too kind to me.

"What was I *thinking*?" I say again.

"I don't know," says Dr. Keats. "What *were* you thinking?"

Dear Earth,

This is what I was thinking: I was about to finish school with the most nugatory degree I could conceive of. I had a not-as-good-as-I'd-hoped short novel coming out with an indie press that was one step up from the Xerox machine at the 7-11 down the street. I was unemployed and probably unemployable. I was single and probably un-de-singleable, and going to the moon was the one thing I'd wanted most since looking up at the night sky as a child and seeing it there, resting matte gold on the horizon or suspended burnished silver at its zenith.

So what do you do when the big news is that they're looking for professional writers to live on the new lunar station and file regular reports, to chronicle the majestic adventure of humanity's first permanent space colony, to write a record to live for the ages?

You polish your CV, one-inch your margins, and you apply for that motherfucker.

You don't actually expect to be *chosen*. You don't expect to ... to have to leave everything behind.

Jamie Oakener was the only person to show up at my first reading, and even that was just a coincidence.

The two-by-five foot foamcore reproduction of my book's cover—its title, *The Thermodynamics of Love* (holy Lord, what was I thinking?), in round, red sans serifs over a picture of some girl much prettier than me looking all heartbroken—is 100 percent of the publisher's marketing budget for the season, and it leans against the front of the little table where I sit, hiding my Levi's legs and the fifty copies of my book that I brought with me from home, and it's the first time in my life that I feel like I might have been too optimistic.

Around two dozen chairs stare me down in the bookstore with a collective ass population of precisely zero. It's twenty minutes past when I'm supposed to start reading, but I'll be damned if I read to no one. Instead I brandish my best passive-aggressive smile at the customers who walk past while avoiding my eyes, a better advertisement for my dentist than for my publisher or myself, probably.

And but so then this girl—all skinny arms and legs, hair a cascade of dark coffee curls, in a blue dress with white polka dots, a string of imitation pearls around her neck—appears, comes straight toward me, and sits down in the front row. Looking just like she walked out of a speakeasy circa 1922. Looking just like she's there on purpose.

And *Dear Earth*, is she ever pretty.

And I say hi and she says hi. And I say, "Do you want to get a cup of coffee?" And she says, "Aren't you going to read?" And I give the empty-but-for-her chairs a declarative look and I say, "It doesn't seem like it."

"Did you actually come here to hear me read?"

And she says, all bashful, "No. You just looked so sad and cute."

So my sad, cute heart does a flip in her direction, and I say again, "Let's get some coffee."

We have the first conversation I have with everybody, which is about my name: how my parents' surname was Tenth, so when I was born on the tenth of December, they thought they'd be all clever and call me December Tenth. I tell this story a lot.

But she does something unexpected. She says, "I have a weird name too!"

"Jamie Oakener?" She's already told me. "What's so weird about that?"

She smiles like a conspiracy.

"Jamie comes from Jameson, which is what my parents were drinking when I was conceived."

I laugh. "Gross!"

"It gets better. I have middle names. My mum's maiden name was Parker, right, and my dad's grandmother's name was Dorothy. Making me—"

"Jamie Dorothy Parker Oakener!" I shout, delighted, informing the whole café, but I don't even care.

"December Tenth," she giggles. "Use your indoor voice!"

The first time I come over, it's raining, and in the morning we sit in the garden drinking coffee and reading the brand new IKEA catalogue to each other and gently waving away the bees that try to land on us because we're so bright and sweet together they mistake us for flowers.

$$\left(\!\!\left(\right.\right.$$

Dear Earth,

The station's electricity is generated in two ways. The first is solar. Because there's no atmosphere beyond our metal-and-plexiglass enclosure, there's nothing to dilute the sun's energy as it reaches the craggy grey surface, so the solar collectors work at almost 100 percent efficiency.

The other way is hydrogen fuel, which we get from mining the ice. Every day a dozen robots roll down into the polar crater below us and come back a few hours later hauling big pyramids of dirty ice. From the area above the vehicle storage unit—the garage, where I am now—you can see them. Robots like a baby elephant crawled inside R2-D2 and had a baby with a Zamboni. Robots crawling up the side of the crater like Sisyphus.

This is how we get our oxygen, too. By a process of electrolysis, the water-ice is split into hydrogen and oxygen: the hydrogen goes into the fuel cells, and the oxygen goes to the generators to produce breathable air. The sighs of the station's 108 personnel make their way to the garden for the plants. The rest of the water is treated and mineralized and fluorinated and made potable for us and for the plants, and our waste water is recycled.

The gravity ... I haven't got even the fuzziest idea about how the gravity works.

In the station, Captain Wallace is in charge. Captain Wallace looks just like an astronaut from a 1950s science-fiction movie: a crew-cut black like oil, eyes blue as Earth and always looking into the distance at something you can't see, like cats do. He's thirty centimetres bigger than me in every direction, and he wears his US Air Force uniform every day, with the silver double-bars of his rank pinned to his lapel. Anytime he's not talking to you, he absently worries the wide gold band around the hairy knuckle of his left ring finger. I'm pretty sure he doesn't realize that he does this. But it makes him seem human to the rest of the crew, rather than like the intimidating, unrelatable archetype he'd otherwise be.

Okay, he is still *kind of* intimidating.

I say, "Good afternoon, Captain." You have to call him Captain. You do not call him Dave. You especially don't do your best HAL 9000 impression when he's around.

"Good afternoon, Ms. Tenth," he says, and even though I've just walked up out of nowhere, he does not startle, and he doesn't turn to look at me, just continues watching, through the window of the garage, the barren crater as the robots return with our water and power and air for the next week. He says, "I read your last transmission to Earth."

Of course he did. Part of his job is reading everything I write and approving or rejecting each post before dispatching it. This is still a military mission, technically, and we can't have me giving away any secrets. Captain Wallace knows all about embedded journalists and their loose lips; he was in the war.

"Did you like it?" I ask.

"It was very ... " His Bruce Campbell chin rises up almost imperceptibly. "*Personal.*"

"Is that bad?"

"No," he says. "No." Out there, the little robots drag their frozen cargo back home, dutiful as ants. Out there, the robots don't remember. Out there, the robots don't dream.

For most of my life on Earth, I felt safe. Safe like a prison is safe. Earth has everything you need to be alive: air, water, food. It's all just there. But the same gravity that keeps the atmosphere from floating away also keeps you rooted to the spot. You look up at the sky at night and what you see is possibility. What you see is freedom. What you see is *everything else*. I always thought that if I went to the moon, I would feel what I never felt down on the planet where I was born. And wouldn't you know it, Earth—I was right.

Here I do feel free. Free, and constantly afraid. This place is hostile. If you want to eat, if you want to *breathe*, you have to come prepared with the products of thousands of years of human civilization strapped to your back. The moon is a blank white page on which we're still scrawling the very first sentences, and we can write anything we can imagine. But while it often feels like Earth is unconcerned with our struggles, the moon's indifference seems to border on the passive-aggressive. On Earth you could always get hit by a bus or eaten by a crocodile—there's never any guarantees, but on the moon you might wake up with a chest full of emptiness and die of suffocation one morning because some asteroid looked at your bedroom the wrong way.

Point being, you think you have to choose. You think it's either safety and confinement, or freedom and fear. You think it can only ever be one way or the other.

Dear Earth, let me count the ways.

The way we have the same arms. The way her socks never match. The way she calls people by their full name. The way the sound of hers, her name, liquefies my heart still. The way she shakes her hair. The way she draws dinosaurs. The way her red nail polish is always perfectly chipped. The way that she's better than me at everything, and the way that makes me feel not envious but proud. The way she'll smile kindly and call you a doofus only when she's really, really mad at you.

Captain Wallace's arms fall back down to his sides, then his hands join behind his back. He looks like he's seen things you people wouldn't believe, like he's thinking deep thoughts, like he's about to say something profound. He kind of always looks like that.

What he says is "Ms. Tenth." What he says is "Being apart from someone, even being half a million miles away, shouldn't make you feel so all alone. It should make you feel *blessed* to live in a universe so kind that it contains a person so special, a person worth missing like that."

Out there, the north stretches across empty space. Out there, the Earth hangs suspended on nothing. Out there in the sky, looking so small and so close that I could reach out and grab it, is everywhere I have ever been.

Standing just behind him, I look at Captain Wallace's hands, holding each other behind his back. He never looks at me, but he unclasps his hands, takes the gold ring on his left hand between two fingers on his right, and turns it round and round like the orbit of the moon.

☾

Dear Earth,

Jamie Oakener came with me to Florida, where the space ships depart, to see me off. It was hot in Orlando. Or it might have been the coldest day in a century, I don't really remember. I think it was raining, though, or snowing maybe, because I do recall that our faces were wet.

We stood close, and she said, "Don't go."

And I said, "Come with me."

"Don't go."

"Come with me."

I looked into her eyes, but I couldn't see a fucking thing.

And she looked into my eyes, and she smiled so kindly, and she said, "You doofus."

Design Flaw

1:

Nerds are all filthy perverts, make no mistake. Don't let the glasses and the shy demeanour fool you; these are the guys who never got laid in high school, and they're severely twisted up about it. Call it a stereotype if you want, but it's true. Get a bunch of nerds together in one place—a game of Dungeons and Dragons, a comic convention, or, in this case, a robotic combat competition—and then drop in a cute girl (a *kawaii otaku* chick, to use their lingo) and watch the geeks descend on her like a pack of rabid wolverines. Mechanical ones. From space.

They're shameless. They'll try anything. Give you chocolate. Offer to help realign your wheel assembly. Tell you that your eyes are the colour of stainless steel. Like that would impress anyone. Frankly, it's just creepy, okay?

It's like, dude, lay off.

I'm *thirteen*, asshole.

2:

The screws are coming loose. I can finally see it all; I can see inside and underneath what everyone else sees, and what I see is that it's all falling apart. I used to suspect, sometimes, but now I know for sure. It's so obvious—it's like I have X-ray vision. Maybe I do. That would make sense. I am machinery just like all the rest of it. The trees, they're clockwork.

You think because you plant a seed and water it and it grows that it's something organic, but it isn't. It's self-replicating, hydraulically powered, maybe nanotechnology. If I hold my ear up to a tree trunk, for all its apparent greenness, I can hear the clicking and ticking of gears inside. The sun up there, just a supraorbital autonomous nuclear fusion power plant. And the people, all robots. Just like the ones that I build. Only more sophisticated. Walking around, carrying out their programming. They think they know what they are, but they don't. They're wrong, all so wrong. This isn't some metaphor. I'm seeing the world for the first time, and it's made of metal.

I crouch down in the grass. I grab a handful of it and pull it up by the roots. They're wires. The green stuff on top is just insulation and photon collectors. Under that, below the surface, it's fibre optic cable and carbon core conductors sparking with electricity. I toss it down and dig into the earth. The dirt isn't dirt. It's all nuts and bolts, microchips piled thousands of kilometres deep. The planet is a giant gravity generator, an enormous spaceship taking us across the universe, delivering us who knows where. All of us robots. How did I not see this before?

And who made it? Who put us here? And what happened to them, where are they now? I see a mechanical squirrel carry a lug nut up to the top of a laser-guided poplar, and I know we've been abandoned. Something has gone wrong; the screws are coming loose, and I'm the only one who knows. It's all up to me. The world is broken. I have to fix it.

I grab my toolbox and run.

3:

Round one is about to begin, and I haven't slept in ninety-six hours. My dad is off checking the battery connectors once more because they came loose in our last practice battle, and we don't want it to happen again. This is the real thing.

We're Team Triforce, my dad and me. He's an engineer. We were watching this show, this robotic combat competition, and I said it would be cool to build our own fighting robot. He thought so too. So we did. It cost a couple of thousand dollars and a year of hard work, and ours is still one of the cheapest bots in the arena today. But I think we've got a good chance at winning.

Triforce is our bot. Everyone asks if my dad built it and I just drive it (that's been the favourite pick-up line of the forty-year-old sickopaths this weekend), but we built it together. My dad named it (after the magical thingy from the *Legend of Zelda* videogames), but I came up with the original design. It's a couple of triangles piled on top of each other, basically. Hence the name. What it looks like is a light grey triangle (actually a triangular prism, about a yard long and four inches thick), which is the base, under which are the wheels, with a dark grey triangle sitting on top and jutting out on the front side. Mounted on the forward triangle is the weapon; it's a combination of a drill (to puncture the chassis of enemy bots and mess up their insides) and a lifting arm (to, um, lift up enemy bots and flip them over), which also works as a srimech, or self-righting mechanism. That's for letting our bot turn itself right-side up again in case it gets flipped.

It's a pretty good design, if I do say so myself. Triforce is fast and the weapon is powerful. I think we're going to do okay.

It's the beginning of the round. Dad and I are in the roboteers' booth, above one corner of the arena. The creator of the opposing bot is in the booth at the opposite corner. He's a fat guy in his forties wearing a black t-shirt with the initials I.C.E. silk-screened onto it. I.C.E. is the name of his bot, a rectangular deal with a chopping axe mounted on top. The initials stand for Internal Combustion Engine, but he pronounces it like *ice*. Which I think is a pretty lame name for a robot, but whatever.

Our bots are on the arena floor, a couple of dozen feet below us. I pull up the antenna on my remote control as the countdown begins.

Three ... two ... one ... ACTIVATE.

Triforce and I.C.E. run right at each other. A lot of robot battles, the bots will go around in circles for a while, sniffing each other out before they go on the attack. Not this time. We're both trying to get the upper hand early, and that means aggression.

Triforce crashes into I.C.E. and the two bots recoil off each other. I.C.E. brings his axe down, but Triforce is already outside of the weapon's range, and the axe hits the arena floor instead.

Triforce backs up some more and then swoops around to I.C.E.'s side, drill already spinning at full speed. I push the controller, and Triforce drives forward, pounding the drill into I.C.E.'s shiny exterior. It doesn't puncture the chassis, but it does leave a nasty-looking dent.

We've drawn first blood!

We back off again. This time I want to play it a little more coy, so I move off and hug the arena wall for a bit. I.C.E. is pursuing, but I'm faster than he is, and I'm also obviously the better driver. I play cat-and-mouse with him for a while, weaving back and forth while he tries to catch me. He's getting frustrated, and I use this to my advantage; I stop and then back up, and the front of him crashes into the back of me. Triforce's rear is pointed, though, so the front of I.C.E. takes some damage. As fast as I can, I spin around and use the drill on his side again, the same side that I hit before. This time the drill goes right through, and I'm sticking right into him. He can't move sideways, but his greater weight means that he could drag me along if he started going again, so I don't have a lot of time to make my next move. I raise the drill—the hydraulic lifter rises until it's as close to straight up as possible, and I.C.E. is hanging off it like a wounded animal on the tip of a spear.

He's heavier than I am, and I don't want to use too much power carrying him around like this, though it does look cool. He's totally my bitch right now. But my next move could be the decisive one if I pull it off, so I lower the drill in one quick motion, and I.C.E. flies off the end of it, landing ...

Landing upside-down across the arena!

This is awesome! He's splayed like an upturned beetle, wheels spinning frantically. Have I got him?

But no. He raises his axe, and it works as a self-righter, tilting him higher and higher until he falls back down, wheels on the floor, right side up.

Now he looks angry. He takes another run at me, and this time I can't get out of the way fast enough. He crashes into me and drops his axe down, hard. The axe is diamond tipped; it must have cost a fortune. Triforce's chassis is made of aluminum. It's a direct hit. I.C.E.'s axe chops down, rending Triforce's skin, cutting into the mechanics inside.

I can feel it. It hurts.

I.C.E. lifts the axe again, and Triforce goes up with it for a few inches before sliding off and falling back down onto the arena floor with a crash.

I try to move, but nothing happens. I can't go forward. I can't go back. I can't lift the drill. It's stopped spinning. I'm dead.

I'm dead.

It's over.

As the countdown to knockout begins, I start to cry.

Five ... four ... three ... two ... one.

My dad hugs me. Over in the other booth, I.C.E.'s creator raises his stupid fat fists in victory.

4:

No fucking drugs. They tried to give me drugs before. I won't do it. I went crazy for a little while once: I wasn't sleeping, and I wasn't eating, and one day I'd just want to throw myself in front of a subway train, and the next I'd go around with a can of Day-Glo pink spray paint writing lines from *Finnegans Wake* and *The Posthuman Condition* on churches. They wanted me to take these little pills, but I wouldn't, and they couldn't force me, and after a while I felt better again. If I told anyone what I know now, they'd just try to put me on the drugs again. But they wouldn't work anyway. Medicine doesn't work on robots. Robots like me. And everyone else. No wonder I went crazy before. I probably walked under some magnets or something.

Then again, these are the same things they give to everyone. Everyone's on the same Xanax and Zithromax, Valium and Viagra, and it seems to work fine on them, and they're just as mechanical as I am. Maybe the pills are technology too, swarming with nanobots or something, designed to reconstruct and repair from the inside alongside my own autonomic healing apparatus. Either way, I'd better stay away from them. For whatever reason, I'm the only one who can see the screws coming loose. I need this perspective if I'm going to fix everything. And my screwdriver. I'll need perspective and my screwdriver. Which I've got right here in my toolbox.

Like I said, this is no metaphor. It's not like *The Matrix* or something, where the machines are really the Oppressive Chains of Society™ and killing guys in suits symbolizes killing guys in suits. This is the twenty-first century. Irony is dead. Now there's just iron.

5:

Dad is out by the arena watching the rest of round one, but I'm back here in the shop working on Triforce. Poor, mutilated Triforce. My baby. My poor, eighty-pound, aluminum, dead baby.

I'm the only one back here. Everyone else is watching the battle. But I can't watch. I wouldn't be able to see anything through the tears, anyway. On the other hand, I could use the soldering iron in my sleep.

Triforce isn't that badly damaged, really. A lot of his internal wiring was severed by I.C.E.'s axe, but none of the essential components were wrecked. So it's largely superficial, but it looks ugly as hell. Just this long, thin opening right down the middle of him, exposing his innermost parts to the world. I'm sitting on the floor, fixing it, when a shadow comes over me.

It's I.C.E. I mean I.C.E.'s creator, that big old guy. I guess I sort of gasped, so he says, "Oh, sorry. Didn't mean to startle you. I just wanted to tell you that you did a great job out there."

I put the soldering iron down, wipe my eyes, and give my best sarcastic snort. "Yeah, great job. Except for the horrible mutilation and death part."

"No, seriously. You really had me on the ropes there for a while. I was getting pretty nervous. Your biggest problem was that your chassis was too soft. Next time you need stronger armour. But you were fast and manoeuvrable, and your weapon design was extremely original."

"Oh, um. Thanks."

He smiles down at me. It's only then that I realize I've managed to hide myself away in the most inaccessible corner of the place, farthest away from anyone who could hear me if I needed to scream.

Then I think, that's stupid. I'm just being paranoid.

Then he kicks the soldering iron across the floor and bends down, putting his huge hand over my mouth. He puts his other arm across my chest and then lowers himself onto me with all his weight.

Triforce is sitting right beside me. Watching. But he does nothing. He can't. Because I let him die.

6:

I can't fix it. I can see the screws coming loose, but I just don't have the right tools. I'm only making things worse like this. I pull the screwdriver out of the daisy I was attempting to repair and replace it in my toolbox. Whatever robot this garden belongs to will be pissed when he sees it. I was only trying to help. But they won't understand.

I run across the street and into a little restaurant, and I head straight for the washroom. I need to sit down for a while, get a grip on myself. I'm obviously malfunctioning. Hence the unusual degree of self-awareness. None of the other robots feel like this. Clearly there's something wrong with me. My optical sensors are leaking.

A bunch of robots look askance at the girl taking her toolbox into the washroom, but I don't care. I sit down in the stall.

At this point, what I need most is to prioritize. I can't change the world. All I can change is myself. So what's most important right now? What's the biggest problem that I can fix on my own?

My armour. It isn't strong enough. The chassis is too soft. Lets enemy weapons in too easily. It's so obvious. I'm wide open here.

Fine. I mean, let's try to be rational about this.

Maybe I prefer it this way. The world, I mean. That it's technological instead of organic. It was just the shock of finding out like this. No advance warning. But I don't actually mind. I mean, think about it this way: your DVD player doesn't demand that you wait in line with it for popcorn and force you to miss the previews, does it? The toaster isn't interested in discussing its feelings over breakfast. A car might kill you, but it won't break your heart. The only bad machines are the ones that think they're people.

So sitting there on the toilet, I just grab the soldering iron, lower my jeans, and get to work.

Someone Tried to Push Someone Else Out of a Moving Car

SOMEONE TRIED TO PUSH SOMEONE ELSE OUT OF A MOVING CAR. A 2008 silver Ford Focus coupe travelling at sixty-two kilometres per hour northeast on Highway 401. They argued, the two of them, and one attempted to eject the other. They were together. Romantically. Were—maybe still are. The precise status of their current association with one another is at present unknown to me. They were, at the time that the One tried to push the Other One out of the car, in a romantic relationship.

The Other One started it. Or that's what the First One, the driver, claimed. The Other One was the passenger. They were going to a concert. It was Sunday morning, summer, ideal weather and a perfect day for an outdoor music festival, the only reason ever to go to Bowmanville, Ontario.

They were running late. The Driver believed that they were running late and blamed the Passenger for this. The Passenger had taken longer than the Driver to get ready and had also forgotten the tickets at home, necessitating that they turn back to retrieve them, losing somewhere between ten and thirty minutes, depending on which of the two of them you asked. Person One was annoyed, wanting to catch the performance of a certain band that would be on early. In the car, Person One was, according to Person Two, sulking silently in a somewhat passive-aggressive manner, and, when repeatedly prompted, Person One expressed the belief that Person Two had been inappropriately leisurely with regard to preparing to depart, because Person Two did not care for the early-performing band that Person One wished to see, and did not care enough about Person One's desire to see the band in question to expedite said preparations.

As a result, the First Person was driving at a speed described by the Second Person as not only in excess of the posted speed limit (which was, and is, for the record, one hundred kilometres per hour), but (here I quote) "scary." The First Person, while admitting that the vehicle had at the time been travelling above the speed limit, insisted that it was not more than five kilometres per hour faster than one hundred, that it was appropriately in accord with the flow of traffic, and, above all, "not scary." The Second Person does not allow that the First Person is qualified to assert whether or not the speed was scary *to Person Two*, as Person Two's subjective experience of fear is an inherently private phenomenological condition, and if Person Two expresses fear, Person One ought to accept that without requiring a [redacted] electrocardiogram. Person One asks me to implore Person Two (on Person One's behalf) not to embellish for the sake of generating sympathy.

The Other Person asked why, if they were running so very late, did the One Person see fit to stop for coffee, which the First One at the time "would not dignify with a response," though the One Person would later explain that, since they had woken up very early, they both needed coffee to be properly awake for the drive, and, since the One assumed at every moment that the Other was seconds away from being ready to leave, the One did not prepare any coffee at home before they departed.

Now, as you can imagine, the conversation between the two of them—the One insisting that the car's speed was perfectly appropriate, while the Other grew increasingly alarmed—led after a certain period of time to the event in question. When Person Two came to the conclusion that Person One was unlikely to slow to a more reasonable speed, Person Two, unwilling to tolerate the danger for the entire duration of the trip, demanded to be let out of the car. A request that Person One described as "ridiculous."

The argument continued to escalate, the Second Person insisting upon exiting the vehicle and the First Person reiterating the idea's absurdity. Voices rose. Unkindnesses were exchanged. At a certain point, Person One relented. After a fashion.

The Driver in fact did reduce the speed of the car to the aforementioned sixty-two kilometres per hour, disengaged the door

locks on the Passenger's side of the car, and said: "Get out, then."
This, suffice to say, was not what the Passenger had meant at all. The
Driver continued to insist that if the Passenger wished to exit the
vehicle, the Passenger was free to do so—was, indeed, *encouraged* to
do so.

The story here becomes less easy to reconstruct. The Driver claims
to have merely tapped or nudged the Passenger on the elbow, not
applying much force in the direction of the door, which was in any
case closed, a gesture which was, in the Driver's estimation, more of
a rhetorical device. The Passenger, on the other hand, insists that the
Driver reached over and opened the passenger-side door and pushed
the Passenger with force and malice as if to eject the Passenger
from the vehicle entirely, as the highway flew by beneath them at
more than sixty kilometres per hour. It was only, the Alleged Victim
contends, the seatbelt that prevented a death, or at the very least
grievous bodily injury. The Alleged Assailant maintains that this
narrative is pure horsefeathers (though "horsefeathers" was not the
precise word used to describe it).

At any rate, following this dramatic peak or culmination of the
event under discussion, whatever it in reality was, things calmed
down, the point having, as it were, been made. Both occupants of
the car in question attended the music festival and remained sedate
throughout, never expressing any actual enjoyment. Whether or
not they arrived in time to catch the One Person's preferred early-
performing band was not disclosed to me. Neither could, for the
record, recall any facts about the catalyst band's performance one way
or the other.

Both, however, tasked me with conveying the following
sentiment, each asking me to deliver an identical sentence to the
other: "I miss you."

Tangled Up in Chrome

SO IT TURNS OUT I'M A ROBOT.

I know, right? It's an old story, but you never expect it to happen to you. I was as shocked as anyone. *At least* as shocked as my parents were when I told them. Or as shocked as they seemed to be, anyway.

"Mom, Dad. I'm a robot."

Okay, I guess their immediate reaction can't be described precisely as shock, because at first they had no idea what the crap I was talking about. Or they were pretending not to. My mom put her index finger on her mouth in that way she has when she's trying to figure out which obscure disease the patient-of-the-week on *House* has got.

"Stevie, I'm afraid I don't know what that means," she said.

"What, are you coming out of the closet?" my dad asked.

"No! I'm not *gay*, I'm a *robot*."

"The *vacuum cleaner* is a robot," my mom said. "You are a flesh-and-blood human being. Trust me, I should know; I was there when you were born."

That's what I'd always thought, but now I'm not so sure. My dad also always claimed to have been there when I was born. My mom insists he was watching the NHL playoffs in the hospital lounge, but he says she was just too full of drugs to notice him standing next to her bed. Listening to the game on headphones.

"If this is a joke," my dad said, "then I don't get it."

I wish it *were* a joke. Or something as simple as being gay. Look, I enjoy boobs as much as the next nine-tenths of guys, and significantly more than the remaining one-tenth, but at least homosexuality makes biochemical sense. Probably you're acquainted with at least a few gay people, but who do you know who's a fucking *robot*? My parents would have been shocked at first, and then, once it sunk in, they would have been fine. My mom would have said, "Don't think this means you're exempt from giving me grandchildren!" My dad would have shrugged and then gone back to watching *Desperate Housewives*. Instead, they were wondering if I was having some kind of psychotic break. My friends would have taken me out to Woody's. Where are you supposed to go for your coming-out party if you're a robot, Radio Shack? I'm not even sure if that place is still in business.

So you know that scene in *Terminator 2* where Arnold has to prove to the scientist guy that he really is a killer cyborg from the future? Something like that seemed to be the most reasonable course of action here too. Okay, technically I don't know what exactly happens there because the movie came out when I was like eleven, and I always closed my eyes during that part, but I figured the same principle was at work: *show*, don't tell.

So I did. I took my left ring finger between the thumb and index finger of my right hand, kind of pushed in and twisted, like trying to open a bottle with a child-proof lid. The sound was just like a knuckle cracking, and the finger came loose. I unscrewed it and it came right off. I held the finger in my right hand and sort of waved it around at my parents. Where the finger had been, there was now just a circle of metal at the knuckle, and the same thing on the bottom of the finger itself, little circuit patterns and blinking lights visible if you wanted to look close enough.

Don't ask what I was doing when I figured this out.

My parents didn't say anything. And suddenly I got really scared and upset, and I thought it would be a pretty good idea to leave my parents alone for a little while after that to ... *come to terms* with the situation ... so I decided to take a bit of a walk—okay, a bit of a *run out the door as fast as I could*—since it was a nice day and stuff, plus, I felt like I really needed a cup of coffee as soon as possible, which only raises further questions since what kind of robot has a caffeine addiction? Alcoholism I could understand. At least there's a precedent for that in popular culture.

On my way to the coffee shop, I tried to screw my finger back in. But I couldn't get the, whatever, the *grooves aligned*, at first, and there was another kind of *crack snap* sound, and I felt like I'd caught it in a car door or something. It stayed in, the finger did, and seemed to have the full range of movement, but it really hurt, the knuckle joint just ached electrically when I tried to move it. So of course I kept moving it.

Anyway. At this point I think it's important for me to kind of run down all the possibilities for how this could have happened. I'll make a list. Lists are good. Lists are helpful. Here we go:

How I Spent My Summer Vacation—or WTF, I'm a Robot?!
(A List by Steven C.)

1. My parents are super-scientists who built me in lieu of having a real child and implanted me with false memories. This does not seem exceptionally likely. Of course, none of this seems very likely, so I'm not sure how much my sense of reality and judgment can be trusted at this point. I've been suspending my disbelief pretty high lately. But really, I doubt that either of my parents could have built a functioning robot so indistinguishable from a human that even it couldn't tell the difference. This isn't *Blade Runner*, and I've never had a dream about a unicorn. I mean, my mom is a nice lady and everything, but she can't even knit a blanket that has all the sides even. And my dad is smart, but if he was going to build a robot son, he would have built one that was better at sports.

   a) Which is another thing! If I am this mighty robot how come I'm such an inferior physical specimen? Theoretically my aforementioned *Blade Runner* reference clears that up a little, because (SPOILER ALERT—stop reading now if you haven't seen *Blade Runner: The Director's Cut*—not because I don't want to ruin it for you, but because if you haven't seen it then you're just not a worthwhile enough person to be doing *anything* until you go out and watch it; it's okay, I'll wait … are you back?) Okay, so: Deckard is supposed to be a replicant too, but he still manages to get his ass kicked by practically every other replicant in the movie, even the girls (hot), so we're supposed to understand that different models are built and programmed with different levels of intelligence, physical strength, etc. So I guess that's a resolvable problem.

2. I was born human, but at some point the original me was replaced with a robot duplicate. This potentially solves the problem of why my parents seemed so surprised to learn I wasn't human. If they were not the ones who built me to replace their son who died/was kidnapped/whatever (though there's precedent for that too: there's that one episode of *Star Trek: The Next Generation* where Data's deceased creator Dr. Noonien Soong's ex-wife shows up, and it turns out that *she's* an android too, because the original human version of her died in an accident, so Dr. Soong built a new one and implanted it with all the original's memories so it didn't even know it wasn't the real her. That was a pretty good episode, actually. Then there was Kubrick and Spielberg's *A.I.* of course, which I think I was the only person in the world who actually liked, but maybe that makes sense too now that I know I'm a machine. Huh.) then it would understandably be kind of a bombshell.

a) So if I'm assuming that my parents genuinely didn't know about this—because it would have been a lot easier just to come clean with it than to act like I brought home some underage runaway pregnant with a litter of puppies—then who *is* responsible?

    i.   Random super-scientist guy. Maybe I got hit by a car and killed when I was a kid, and behind the wheel was a crazy-brilliant engineer who, rather than face the music, decided to create an exact duplicate of me and release it back into the wild.

    ii.   Aliens. Hell, why not? They abducted the original human me and replaced me with a robot clone—what, to conduct surreptitious surveillance? I think they'd be able to find a better candidate for artificial impersonation than me. I'm not exactly privy to any useful information, other than the secret recipe for the greatest motherfucking grilled cheese sandwich on earth … okay, this idea suddenly got a lot more plausible.

    iii.   Time travellers from the future. I don't know why I think this is the best option so far, because seriously why would anyone from the future want to replace me? It just seems like something that future-people might do. Don't you think? They're probably really bored in the future, what with us already having done absolutely everything that it's scientifically possible to do by the early twenty-first century. Maybe interfering with the past is the only way to kill time after the End of History.

3. Time-travelling aliens drunk-driving their spaceship struck and killed me and built a robot replacement to throw the authorities off their ion trail.

4. Or my mom had an affair with the vacuum cleaner. Let's not think too hard about this one.

Those are all the possibilities I can imagine right now. At least until I've had some coffee.

I go up to the counter, and the cute, chubby black girl with a mohawk behind it asks me what I want, and I tell her, blah blah blah, I get my coffee and go sit down. Well, it's not quite that simple because actually the place is full, and I have to wait a million years before there's a vacant table, but that allows me to hang out uncomfortably here and steal surreptitious glances every now and then at the girl behind the counter; have you ever noticed that baristas seem to be an average of thirty-eight percent more attractive than the random girls you see just walking around (and possibly the random guys as well, but I couldn't verify that statistic personally)? I'm not sure what that's about. Maybe it's because they're specially trained by the Caffeine Overlords to be nice and obsequious to customers so that you'll buy the more expensive drinks in a misguided attempt to impress them with your affluence, or so that you'll come back instead of just making coffee at home. Or maybe it's how they call you "sir."

This other girl enters the place and heads straight for the counter; the barista's eyes and mouth go all wide as she obviously recognizes her friend.

"Oh my gosh!" she says, as her friend runs up and grabs both her hands across the counter. "I have to tell you about this dream I had about you last night! This ... *lesbian* dream."

Or maybe it's that.

I don't know what a robot needs with a sex drive anyway. Presumably robots can't reproduce. Seems kind of counterproductive if you ask me. Counterreproductive.

A seat finally becomes available (though not one of the big purple floofy ones, dammit—just a regular wooden one at a small round table full of napkins wet with spilled Pike Place blend) and I sit down with my coffee. The next few minutes are not very interesting, so I'll spare you the details. Lots of sipping and sighing, is all.

But then someone pulls out the chair across the table from me, and I look up, startled. He's older, maybe fifty, maybe sixty, wearing a waistcoat and—I swear—a *trilby hat*, with greying sideburns poking out from under it. He looks familiar.

"Can I sit down?" he says.

And I go, "Holy crap, you're me."

He says, "I'll take that as a yes," and he sits down across from me, and I notice that suddenly this is the only occupied table in the whole place—everyone else left while I was sitting here sulking. Even the big purple floofy chairs are vacant. Son of a bitch.

"I'm glad you figured it out so quickly," he says. And yet, to make sure that I absolutely grok the situation, he says, "Steven ... I'm you from the future."

"If you're from the future," I say, "then why are you dressed like it's 1922?"

And he says, "Uh, because it's *awesome*?"

That's me, all right.

"Don't talk," he says, "just listen. I'm not the you that you're going to become. I'm the original you. I was taken by agents from the future and hidden, replaced by a perfect robot duplicate—that's you. They needed to protect me because there's going to be an ... incident ... in several years, an incident that has to occur for various reasons, but which also would have killed me in the process, which must *not* happen, for the sake of the future of humanity. I can't tell you exactly what it is, but you'll know it when you see it. No human could survive it, but you will. Then we'll switch places again: you'll go into hiding and hang out with the future people, and I'll come back and resume my life. It's a *Prince and the Pauper* sort of deal. It's a bit complicated. But the gist of it is *you are the most important person in the world*."

Yeah, no, that didn't really happen. The part about being a robot is true, but I daydreamed that last bit. With the me from the future and the being important. Sorry. Really I'm still just sitting here drinking coffee, and the barista is chirping to her friend about something that I suspect would be of great interest to me if I could hear it, and some very loud and annoying guys are sitting in the big, comfortable, floofy chairs where I would be if there were any justice in this world. That would have been cool though, right? Guy from the future shows up and explains everything? Here's something else that didn't happen but would be pretty great if it did:

Loading Super Robot Battle ...

The glass doors of the coffee shop explode inwards, and a giant evil robot stomps through the frame and commences wrecking up the place. It's not giant giant, not Mechagodzilla huge, but it's pretty big. Like, if ED-209 is a Cadillac Escalade, this thing is a Honda Element. Smaller and slightly less obnoxious, but equally ugly and evil.

People hide under their tables, five-dollar drinks spilling everywhere. I, however, leap to attention. To the rescue. Innocents are threatened, and if it's a robot that's doing the threatening then it stands to reason that a robot will do the rescuing too.

"Out of the way!" I shout (to the humans). Utilizing my superior robotic strength (don't worry about what I said before about being an inferior physical specimen; let's say I was being modest) I pick up the chair I'd been sitting in and hurl it at the Big Guy's face ... er ... its, you know, *robo-face*. It rotates its upper chassis so that its optical sensors face the incoming projectile. A blood-red beam of energy emerges from it, accompanied by a loud buzz like a refrigerator with rabies. Its aim is perfectly calibrated, and the chair, struck in mid-air by the bright crimson laser, instantly disintegrates into a filthy cloud of smoke. An unexpectedly thick forest-fire smell fills the café.

This is merely a diversionary tactic. While the Mechanical Maniac is distracted by the chair, I execute a jet-powered slide across the grey tiled floor. Its vision momentarily disrupted by the smoke from the destroyed chair, it doesn't detect me moving toward it; I close the distance between the two of us in a split second and complete a swirl-kick to the thing's right leg, knocking it off balance. It tilts off its axis, totters, and then tumbles sideways, crashing to the ground, denting the floor with a crater due to its enormous weight.

It's not yet defeated, but then I notice something: while all the patrons of the coffee shop have managed to escape through the shattered door, the barista hasn't; she appears to be trapped behind the counter, her escape route probably blocked, because she's just standing there, surveying the scene, and not even attempting to run. Paralyzed with fear, perhaps.

I run back the length of the room and leap over the counter with a mid-air double forward flip. Could have gone around it instead, I guess, but I'm in a double-forward flipping sort of mood now. I curl my arm around the girl—let's call her Alexis, since that's what her nametag says—and heroically declare, "Come on, I'm getting you out of here."

She smiles on just the left side of her face.

"Oh yeah?" she says, and then raises her right hand parallel to her body. She makes a fist, and suddenly her entire hand sinks down and disappears into her sleeve; the mouth of an ion-cannon emerges, Mega Man styles. I'm dumbstruck! I take a second look at her nametag: it doesn't say *Alexis* after all. Actually, it says *ALEX-15*.

At last: a compatriot.

That would be neat, huh?

For real, though, nothing like that ever happens. I don't know. What really happens is that I finish my coffee and go back home.

Descartes had a thing about robots. (How's that for a science-fiction reference?) He'd be all sitting at his desk and would look out the window and see a bunch of people walking down the street outside, and they'd all look completely identical, with their hats and their umbrellas, and it made him wonder why he thought that they were people at all. I don't think he actually used the word *robots*, but that's the kind of thing he was talking about. Mechanical humans. How do any of us know that other people are really people at all? We think we know what we are, and we just go on to assume that everything out there that looks or acts the way that we do probably is just like us, with reasoning and feelings and hopes and fears and beliefs and, you know, *a mind*. Then it turns out that you're not actually what you thought you were after all—instead, some anonymous force went and constructed you in a factory in space or whatever, who knows why— and then what the hell are you supposed to do?

When I get home, my parents are sitting in the kitchen. They're drinking coffee. Instant coffee. My mom's is decaf because that's all she drinks. They look up when I walk in, and I've obviously caught them in the middle of a very important discussion. Probably they're trying to decide which insane asylum or government agency to send me to. I hear DARPA is nice this time of year.

But my mom says, "Stevie. Sit down." And she sounds calm and caring. My dad pushes out a chair for me. So I sit.

"Sorry we were so ... that we reacted so badly before," my dad says. He doesn't say sorry very often, so this is a pretty big deal.

"It's okay," I say. "It's a lot to deal with."

"Well, in a way, yes," my mom says. In a way? "This isn't something that we were prepared for you to find out just yet, to be honest," she says. This jars me.

"You *knew*?"

My parents look at each other then back to me, and they nod.

"How long have you known?" I say. "Why didn't you tell me? How did this happen? Why am I like this? Aliens? Super-scientist? Time travel? What?" Funny how it takes me two seconds to say out loud what it took me an hour to figure out for myself. My parents look at each other again. Then they both lay down their left hand on the table in front of them. I don't know what they're doing. But then they both take their other hand and use it to grab the fingernail of the ring finger on their left, both of them, the finger they wear their wedding rings on. They each pull on the fingernail gently, and it lifts up, opens like a trap door. And underneath, in the nail bed, there's metal. Circuits and LEDs.

I more or less totally lose my shit.

"You're robots? I mean, we're all—what the crap is going on here? Why didn't you—"

"It's complicated, Stevie," my mom says. She and my dad both put their fingernails back, which is good because it was kind of creeping me out.

"It was a pretty big surprise," my dad says. He then realizes that he pretty much just told me I was an accident and looks contrite. I don't really care. He goes on. "We both had figured out what we really were, independently. We never told anyone else. But when we met in university and decided we wanted to get married, we each thought it was important that the other know what was really going on."

"It was kind of funny," my mom adds. "Your father said, 'I have something I have to tell you,' and I said, 'There's something I have to tell you too,' and he said, 'Me first,' and I said, 'No, me first,' and it was all very romantic-comedy of us." They smile at each other.

My dad continues, "It was definitely weird, but we both figured that we'd met for a reason, somehow. It was just too strange to have been a coincidence, right? Two robots, meeting, falling in love? At random?"

"We didn't think that we could have children," my mom says. "But we did. I got pregnant, and you were born just like any other baby. But you were like us. It was ..."

She trails off, and my dad picks it up.

"Miraculous," he says.

"Miraculous," my mom agrees.

"But where did you *come from*?" I say. "Robots don't just ..." I make a gesture with both my hands to try to indicate popping into existence *ex nihilo*, but it probably looks more like an octopus indecently exposing itself. "Robots are *built*, someone *builds* robots. So who ... I mean ... where did we come from, why are we here?"

My parents give each other that look again.

"We don't know," my dad says.

"Stevie," my mom says, "you're going to have to figure out your own life for yourself, but what we decided, the two of us, your father and I, is that ... however this happened, it happened. We're here. Your father and I are here for each other, and we're here *for you*."

That is such a my mom thing to say, by the way. She can be very *movie-of-the-week* sometimes.

So my parents didn't make me the way I'd always thought they had, but then again, they sort of did. And someone or something must have made them too, not in the usual way, maybe the same way as I was, and then again maybe not. How far back does this go? How the hell could I possibly find out? It's just ... it's just what I said. Robots are built, manufactured. Confused as I am, of this I'm sure. Robots don't just ... you know?

At this point it feels like my brain is spinning around inside my head—and who knows, maybe it actually is; I don't know if my brain is like a flash drive or HDD or what—and I really just get this very strong desire not to be talking about it anymore.

So I say, "I need some time to ... to process this." I'm sounding like a robot. I almost said "does not compute." Really getting in touch with my heritage, here.

"Great," says my dad, who enjoys discussing emotional stuff like this even less than I do. "Hockey game's on. Want to watch?"

I say, "Absolutely." My mom gives me a hug. I curl my right hand around my left ring finger, which still really hurts, actually, hasn't stopped hurting this whole time, and just hold it like that for a little while. On the way down to the living room, though—because, you know, who knows—I still shoot a dirty look at that smug bastard of a vacuum cleaner.

The Middle of Things
or
1922 and All That

IT'S A BOOKSHOP, BUT IT'S ALSO A PRIVATE LIBRARY, AND AS OF THIS week it's a publishing company too, but mostly it's the best place in the world if you're alive and you want to meet everyone who made English literature habitable for the last century. It'll be another several decades before I'm born but never mind that; what matters is that I'm here now (or "was there then," if you prefer), and it's so exciting that I just might swoon. I'm pretty sure that swooning is era-appropriate here. Or am I too late for that? Swooning is a sort of nineteenth-century affectation, isn't it? No, wait, people swooned for the Beatles, and they're still almost half a century away. In my day, no one ever swoons except maybe ironically. But no one really does anything except ironically in my day. Which is why my day isn't as good as this one right here. If you see what I mean.

Anyway. Here on the Left Bank is where all the expat-Anglos stay, and a couple years back this American woman, Sylvia Beach, opened an English-language bookstore to make it easier for everyone to get the British and U.S. literary mags, plus all the canonical English lit you might want. She called it Shakespeare and Company, and sitting there in the window when I come up to the place are great big, beautiful editions of Chaucer, Shakespeare of course, and a copy of Jerome K. Jerome's *Three Men in a Boat*, which I've always meant to read but never got around to. Gotta remember to take it out of the library when I get back to the future. I love saying that. *Back to the future.*

I'm stalling, hanging around out front, staring in the windows. No sense in getting discouraged now. It's chilly; it's February in Paris after all, so that's the other reason I've got cold feet. All I've got to do is open the door and walk inside. I can do this. No, seriously.

The door opens and someone walks out, and I use the unexpectedness of the event to spur myself on. I stumble forward one step then another, and the next thing I know, I'm inside. I'm *inside* Shakespeare and Company. The real one, the original. Shelves and tables full of books, photographs of writers lining the walls, a heating stove to keep us from freezing. Holy crap.

It's early in the morning, though I'm not sure exactly what time. Wristwatches (pocket watches too, which I guess is probably what they've got here), as a rule, tend to be composed not insignificantly of metal, so they can't make it through time transit. Organic stuff only. God knows why. Something about the photoelectric effect, some people think. I don't really know what that is. There's a lot about time travel that nobody understands, even the ones who invented it. But it's not much of a problem: my suit is cotton, my hat is fur, my shoes are leather. No dental fillings or cybernetic implants. I'm looking pretty spiffy, if I do say so myself. Very *period*. I mean, it had better look good. Time travel isn't cheap; you're already paying I'd-be-embarrassed-to-tell-you-how-much for a jaunt to the Roaring Age, and you don't want to skimp on the details for when you actually get there. You know, you don't want to look like some kind of ... *tourist*. The point is, it's early, so there isn't much of a crowd. Just a couple of people milling around, checking out the shelves, nobody I recognize, but both of them periodically travelling back to the front counter to talk to—oh.

Oh. Oh, oh, oh, it's her! It's Sylvia! I mean, I knew she would be here, but ... I think this is the point where the swooning occurs. She sees me. She smiles. She calmly comes over and greets me. What.

Her eyes are brown and bright and make her look friendly and welcoming beyond reason. They shine when she smiles. Her hair is brown too, thick and wavy and shoulder length, and she's wearing a brown velvet jacket, which looks really fantastic on her even though I usually hate brown clothes, as a rule. She's not pretty, exactly, but there's still something alluring about her. Not just her reputation. I suspect that it's the other way around: she gained her reputation by being the sort of person that it's impossible not to trust at first sight.

"Hello," she says. "I haven't seen you in here before. I'm Sylvia, the owner."

I introduce myself, almost extending my hand to her but then reconsidering—do men and women shake hands in this era? Anyway, my palms are so sweaty that I wouldn't give a very good impression, even if they did. She doesn't seem to be offended.

"Pleased to meet you," she says. Oh, I love her already. This is too much. "Are you staying in Paris?" she asks. "Visiting? Where are you from?"

I tell her "I'm from the future" because what the hell.

"That so?" she says. Not one beat missed. This is a lady at the absolute top of her game. "How far in the future?"

Turns out I'm the one who loses my cool—me, the cynical twenty-first century guy. Now, this is my first trip through time, but all those science-fiction movies always warned against polluting the timeline with information from the future, warned not to disclose your true origin and whatever. In real life, none of that matters. First thing they realized when they started sending people back was that you can't make any big changes, no matter how hard you try. Little things can change, but the continuum always compensates for any major fuckery. Either events beyond your control will prevent you from doing what you want, or else the universe heals itself around the wound, and when you get back to where you came from, things are pretty much the same as when you left.

Time transit is mostly used for scientific research, but if you're a civilian with a couple hundred million dollars lying around, you can get yourself a ticket to ride. A few people paid astonishing amounts of money to go back and kill Hitler, of course; one guy intended to give Archduke Ferdinand a little heads-up. They disappeared in the accelerator like they were supposed to, but just never came back. Nobody knows what happened to them. Maybe they died, maybe they ended up in some parallel universe, but they just vanished, and as far as anyone can tell nothing changed. Not that we'd know if anything *did* change, since we'd be affected along with the rest of the universe if the timeline were re-written. But I mean, I still know who Hitler is, and it's not some guy who was assassinated by a billionaire software engineer from the future, unfortunately, so we tend to assume that it didn't work out.

"Uh, about a century, give or take," I stammer. I don't know why her being so casual left me so nonplussed, but there you go. Maybe I just enjoy shocking people. "You don't sound very surprised," I say.

She actually winks at me.

"The first time I met Hemingway, he told me that he'd slept with Mata Hari," she says. "If you've got a good story, I'm certainly not going to give you any trouble."

What a doll, right?

"Much appreciated," I say.

"So what can I do for you?" she asks.

"I'd like to purchase a copy of *Ulysses*."

"Excellent choice. Out of print in the future, is it?"

"Not at all," I say. "Quite the contrary." She looks cheered by this, almost like she actually believes me. "But it's not for me," I continue. "It's a gift for someone. Someone from the past. I mean, from the present. You know. Today."

"Lovely," she says. She goes and retrieves a copy of *Ulysses*. There's a thousand pages of it, and its cover is a deep shade of blue, like the flag of Greece. She gives it to me. I take it. I'm holding it in my hands, a brand-new first edition of the greatest novel of the twentieth century, which Sylvia Beach took a chance on and published at her own expense because no one else would. I almost drop it. It's heavier than it looks.

I thank Sylvia and pay for the book, which costs less than a good cup of coffee back home.

"Just one more thing," I say. "I wonder if it might be possible to, uh, have it inscribed. By the author."

Sylvia chuckles.

"Joyce would be happy to inscribe it for you, I'm sure. He usually comes in late in the afternoon to ransack the place."

"I'm afraid I don't have that much time," I say. "I have a train to catch."

"Oh, a time train?" Sylvia says. "How exciting."

"Just a regular train," I say. "I'm leaving for Odessa this evening."

"You're quite an adventurer," Sylvia says. "Well, there's a good chance that Joyce will be lunching with his family at Michaud's. You could see if you can find him there."

I love how *lunch* is a verb here.

"Thank you so much," I say. I tip my hat to her, and then wonder if it was improper to have left it on my head when I entered the store

in the first place. Manners! Nobody worries about stuff like that when
I come from. In the future, shopkeepers are ecstatic as long as you
don't steal anything or take a leak on the floor. "It was absolutely an
honour and a pleasure meeting you," I say.

"Likewise, I'm sure, Mr. Time Traveller. Tell me," she says
indulgently, "do you have any advice from the future that might be of
some benefit to a simple bookshop owner of the 1920s such as myself?"

And again, I think, what the hell. I say, "Yeah. Watch out for
the Germans."

"Well," she says, "I knew *that* already."

As I arrive at Michaud's, James Joyce is just leaving. Which is
convenient because I really wouldn't have liked to disturb him during
his meal. Probably would have ended up as some jerk who interrupts
HCE as he dines with his family in *Finnegans Wake*. Actually, that
would be awesome. Why couldn't I get here a few minutes earlier? I
got lost. Damn my non-existent sense of direction. Guess I was lucky
to have found the place at all; I can barely navigate my own city in
my own century even with the GPS built into my handheld. Oh well.

The first thing I notice about him is his delightfully ridiculous
Modernist facial hair: a thin moustache paired with a soul-patch kind
of thing, a stripe of fuzz sprouting vertically down his chin from his
lower lip. No one I know could pull off that look with sincerity; on
Joyce it looked silly and great and disarmed me immediately. Besides
that, he's wearing a dark blue suit, black felt hat pushed to the back
of his head, and the lenses in his glasses are mismatched: the left one
is normal, but the right is much thicker and darker, almost sunglass-
like. I knew that he'd had chronic glaucoma and several eye operations
and was nearly blind in his right eye. He strolls casually away from the
restaurant, twirling a wooden cane. On his feet, clashing wonderfully
with the otherwise semi-formal attire, a pair of sneakers that had
probably been white once.

With him is his family. His wife, Nora: tall, with curly red hair. And
his children, Giorgio and Lucia, running in circles around their parents'
feet and whispering to each other. I regard Lucia dolefully. She'll grow
up frightfully schizophrenic, spending most of her life in an asylum,
dying there. Today, though, she's looking happy and robust.

Swallowing my anxiety, I step in front of them, holding out my hand to the author.

I say, "Pardon me. Is this the great James Joyce?"

Flattery never hurts, and anyway it's true. He bows his head humbly and, reaching out to grasp my hand in his, says, "James Joyce." His voice is much higher pitched than I'd expected. But in a charming way, not grating. And, of course, with a soothing Irish lilt to it.

The usual self-effacing and sucking up from me: "It's such an honour to meet you, sir. Terribly sorry to bother you and your family, but Sylvia Beach mentioned I might find you here. I wonder if I might ask you a favour, to inscribe this for me." I hold out the copy of *Ulysses* I'd just bought. He regards it pleasantly, I think. He smiles at me.

"For a friend of Sylvia's, anything," he says, and I have to stop myself from going, "Oh, not a friend, I only just met her today, blah, blah, blah," with stars all up in my eyes. I really don't want to waste too much of his time. He takes the book from me and produces a pen from his suit pocket. Opening it to the first page he asks, "To whom shall I make it out?"

This is the important part, right here. I'd had to figure this out very carefully in preparation for coming here, doing this. Slowly and clearly, I explain exactly what I want him to write. He raises his eyebrows at me, but then nods lightly and writes, precisely how I'd asked.

I gush, "Thank you so much, sir. You have no idea what this means to me."

"That was going to be my question, as a matter of fact," he says, handing the book back. "What *does* it mean, what I wrote there?"

I smile. I can't help it.

I say, "You tell me first."

He laughs, which makes my day ... my century. I thank him again, maybe more profusely than necessary, apologize to his wife for taking up her time, and head out to the train station.

Now this, this is the hard part, right here.

It's a small farm on the outskirts of Odessa, and it takes so bloody long to get to from Paris, first by train, then another train, which seems anachronistically old, like somehow from an era before the invention of the locomotive—reminding me of the time transit accelerator, actually, which is ridiculously high-tech and futuristic while at the same time kind of creepily Victorian. It does feel strangely like getting on a train, travelling through time does, not nearly as science-fictiony as you'd expect. A little science-fictiony, just not as much as you think it's going to be. You walk into the building, and it's this huge, cavernous, oval-shaped domed thing, all marble and iron, four storeys tall, with windows that start about a dozen feet above the ground and just go all the way up. The walls are lined with computer terminals and whatever, but if you're standing in the centre of it, you don't notice them. What you notice is the huge, like, scoreboard thing that rises up from the floor to about one storey into the air, arcane letter-and-number-and-symbol combinations illuminated with LEDs, yellow and red and green, constantly changing, counting up or counting down or just scrolling right to left, like a stock ticker or, yes, train station arrivals-and-departures display, and about equally comprehensible, which is to say equally incomprehensible.

Then you take the elevator down to track level. The time transit accelerator itself is like if a subway and a cyclotron had a baby. The doors slide horizontally open, you get inside the car, and they close again behind you. The car itself is only about half the length of an actual subway car, and there's only a single seat, length of a park bench, at the front. The seat is stainless steel, and it's shiny and slippery, and there's a bar that comes down to restrain you like on a roller coaster.

In front of you is a window the shape of a widescreen TV, probably fifty inches on the diagonal, made of aluminized glass, and it looks out onto the track ahead of you. Out there the only things to see are the laser emitters along the circumference of the tunnel. You can't see the actual laser beams, of course, only the little blue-white and yellow-white glow of the emitters, but there are so many of them, stretching out apparently infinitely ahead of you, that it's as if you're looking up at the stars on a perfectly clear night from the top of a mountain, except they're totally uniformly distributed, the lights, their pattern obsessively invariant, each one perfectly equidistant from every other, which makes it sort of unsettlingly artificial, not actually like the real stars at all, which are comforting and natural and look more like someone casually tossed them down into the firmament just to see where they'd happen to fall, like a handful of crushed limestone.

Then there's a sound like a fridge's compressor clicking on or an air conditioner starting up. And suddenly you're moving forward, and you're accelerating, the points of light out there rushing past you increasingly fast until they're just blurry radiant streaks, the invisible laser beams firing at you, passing through these things called *temporal lenses*, which you also can't see but you know are there, creating an effect that the scientists call *temporal telescoptopy*, but which anyone who's ever time travelled calls *temporal colonoscopy* because, they'll all tell you, what it feels like is you're getting shoved up into the timestream's asshole and are riding round through its spiralling entrails.

I don't know how any of it works, I just read the 'pedia page on time transit on the cab ride over to the accelerator site. But I don't think anyone really knows how it works, no matter what they say. Maybe nobody really knows how or why anything works, and that's not the important part anyway. There's this sensation that's a bit like static electricity and a bit like frostbite, and then a sound like when you shake a handsaw and its blade flexes and bends, and then you, your body and anything non-metallic that you're wearing or holding, and I guess your soul if you think you've got one—though if you're from when I'm from, you probably think you don't, but I figured I'd mention it anyway—you disappear out of the accelerator and reappear somewhen else. Time travellers always get pretty anemic after a jump, so they advise you to eat lots of protein when you arrive. There's a little place I found in Paris that makes a mean steak tartare, which worked for me. I don't remember the name of it, but it burns down twenty-two years later anyway, so, you know.

Uh, where was I? Oh, right. So then after the second train—this is in 1922 again, now—I hire a cart. I'm afraid I'll run out of time and get transmitted back to the future (still cool, that phrase) before I can even do what I came here for, which would suck for a whole lot of reasons. Everything is even more complicated because of the current political situation: post-World War I, post-Bolshevik Revolution, post-Russian Civil War, post-Ukrainian War of Independence and occupation by the French then the Communist Red Army then the counter-revolutionary White Army then finally the Red Army again. So there's a lot of confusion, suspicion, flat-out corruption, and genuine danger, which means that my journey from Paris to here scares me a lot more than my trip back in time did, which was a moonlit gondola-ride in comparison. I have to hand out a lot of bribes, and whenever anyone asks why the hell I would want to go to Odessa now, I have to explain that I'm visiting some relatives. Which is true.

Approaching the farmhouse, I don't see any animals, and the fields are bare ... which could be because of the time of year (I had to acquire a parka-like thing before I left Paris, and I'm deadly glad that I did because it's colder than hell out here) but is equally likely a result of the famine that ravaged the area in the wake of the civil war. Basically the place is just absolutely fucked, and I'm finding it hard to understand how human beings can even live here ... and I have to keep reminding myself not to think about how it's going to get a lot worse long before it gets any better, which some people would argue it never does get, much. Better.

I tighten my parka-thing and go up to the farmhouse door.

I knock. A man opens the door. I say "a man," but he's in his early twenties at best, maybe only as old as the twentieth century itself at this point. Younger than I am. Seems like where I come from—*when* I come from—everything and everyone is just less serious, less real. The past (at least as I've experienced it so far) feels different. Harder, yet somehow finer—the people and things appearing more distinct from their surroundings, if that makes any sense. As if it's easier to apprehend things because time is thicker, maybe, more viscid, or simply flowing slower than I'm accustomed to. It's weird. It's difficult to explain. It's like, you know when you and your friends decide to go out to a bar one night, and you say, "Who's got a car?" and everyone except you raises their hand, and you go, oh shit, my friends are all grown-ups, how did that happen? Yeah, that's what travelling back in time is like.

Anyway, whatever. I greet him with a "Zdravstvuyte," which is even harder to pronounce than it is to spell so don't even bother unless your surname ends with a labiodental fricative. I've never been good with languages, but I took Russian lessons for a year in preparation for this. I doubt I could survive a page of Dostoevsky, but I should be able to make it through the few minutes of informal conversation I'll need here. I hope.

The man regards me with suspicion.

"Can I help you?" he says, except, you know, in Russian.

"I'm a relative," I say. I tell him my name. "Can I come in? A few minutes. It's very cold."

He has no reason to trust me. I could be anybody. There's no KGB yet, but that doesn't mean it's safe to talk to strangers. He weighs the possibilities in his mind for a moment, then opens the door wide enough to let me in. He gestures for me to enter. I do. He shuts the door behind me.

Inside the little farmhouse, there's a wood-burning oven in one corner, and sitting in a not-very-comfortable-looking chair is a woman, the man's wife. A thick grey quilt covers her body. A kerchief wrapped around her head. And in her arms, a baby, a boy, not yet a year old. The child is quiet, not crying at all. The woman sees me and starts to get up.

"No, please," I say, "sit, sit. I only need a minute." I pull *Ulysses* from the depths of my parka-thing. "This is for you," I say, addressing the man again, who looks more confused than ever now.

He takes the book from me. He looks at it, feels its dark blue cover with his thumb. Then he opens it. He examines the inscription.

"I don't understand," he says.

"It's a gift. That's all. For you. For your family."

"But ... English," he says. "I can't read this. I don't know English."

"That's fine. It's a ... " I can't remember how to say *antique* in Russian, but then I realize it isn't really, technically, an antique at all. Yet. "It's rare. It will become valuable."

He nods.

"Thank you," he says. "But please, let me give you something for it."

"No, it's for you. Free, a gift. You owe me nothing, please."

He looks back at his wife, at his son. Then turns back to me. Holding the book, heavy with words and time, with both hands.

"Thank you," he repeats, bowing his head very slightly.

"Thank *you*," I say.

The most direct route from one point in time to another is almost never a straight line. Time is smart. Time notices things. Time has a plan and will make adjustments for unexpected events, for any attempts to short-circuit it. You can't take the obvious path if you want to change history. You have to go around in a spiral, the way time itself moves. Time is subtle. Time likes things to appear accidental, haphazard, even when they're not, *especially* when they're not, like the stars in the sky. Time prefers things to look like a coincidence.

Twenty years from now, when the Romanian military enters the city and commits what becomes known as the Odessa Massacre, both of them, the man and his wife, die. For no reason. Along with about a hundred thousand others. Their son, though, and his brother and sister, who will also be born by then, survive. This house survives. The boy lives through another decade under communism after that, but with the death of Stalin, he escapes to Athens, and from there to Haifa. With him he takes only a single suitcase. Inside, nothing but a few books, his father's books. Scripture, mostly. Not even clothing. It takes the massive bribe of a Soviet official to prevent the suitcase from being tossed into the sea. He becomes a farmer, too, like his father. He gets married, has children of his own.

His son meets a girl at university, a visiting student from *chutz la'aretz*—abroad. He asks her to marry him, and she agrees, but only if he'll return with her to live in Canada. So in 1975, he continues his father's journey west. As a gift on his wedding day, he receives, from his father, some old books from the Old Country. The books have been beautifully kept, taken care of, lovingly treasured for all these years.

Those books live on a shelf in the new house in Montreal. They're there when his own child is born. His son grows up with these books on his father's bookshelf. He can't read them. They're written in Hebrew and in Yiddish and in Russian. And maybe, I hope, one in English. Please, let one of them be written in English. Let one of them be inscribed on the first page, in English, in ink a hundred years old, with a few words, just a couple of simple sentences. Please. Let this kid, living one century, three generations, and half a planet away, take this book off the shelf one day, turn to the first page, and read a handful of script that means nothing to anyone else, has never made any sense to anyone who has ever seen it before him, let this kid read what's written there, and please, *please*, let him understand.

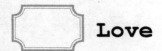 Love

[luhv]
noun
    1. A subcategory of stress.

↑ ↑ ↓ ↓ ← → ← →
B A START

KIDS CALLED IT THE KONAMI CODE, OR SOMETIMES THE CONTRA CODE: a specific pattern of input that, when performed upon the buttons of the console's controllers at the right time, would for certain games— typically those produced by jukebox-rental-outlet-turned-big-deal-digital-entertainment-concern Konami, ergo the cognominal code—give the player some major unfair advantage, allowing him or her well-nigh to waltz effortlessly through stages of the game that may have been difficult unto impossible, as so many of those games were, and for many of us unpassable under normal, unassisted circumstances.

For instance, *Gradius*, first ever occurrence of the Code in a game. In this quintessential 1985 shooter, you control a sixty-seventh century spacecraft and are tasked with the duty of blowing up a bunch of those giant stone heads from Easter Island for some reason, thus saving the galaxy. Entering the Code while the game is paused will instantly activate almost every available power-up, considerably increasing your ship's abilities.

Contra, for the Nintendo Entertainment System, was many players' first exposure to the Code, forever cementing the association between this game series and the Code. In this side-scrolling shoot'em up action game, one of the first console titles to feature a two-player simultaneous gameplay mode, a pair of well-armed commandoes take on a terrorist group bent on world domination. When the Code is entered at the game's title screen, each player is granted thirty lives rather than the usual three, both in the initial game and any subsequent continues.

In *Castlevania: Bloodlines* for the Sega Genesis system, entering the Code confers nine lives upon the player character, John Morris, who uses the legendary Vampire Killer Whip to cut a swath of ruin across a supernaturally infested post-World War I Europe in his quest to hunt down and ultimately destroy the resurrected Count Dracula.

In *House League Peewee Ice Hockey*, using the Code significantly increases your spatial perception and dexterity. This allows you to step out of the way rather than have your teammate accidentally catch the blade of his stick in the blades of your skates, causing you to crash excruciatingly awkwardly to the ice and break your upper femur so badly that it requires two separate surgeries to repair. With the Code that does not happen. By avoiding this event, your movement points are not reduced, so you can skate just like a completely normal, symmetrical adult person for the remainder of the game and spend the rest of the seventh-grade level in high spirits.

In *Teenage Mutant Ninja Turtles IV: Turtles in Time* for the Super Nintendo Entertainment System, when the title screen appears, if you enter the Code on the second-player controller, it gives you ten lives to slice and dice the evil Foot Clan across time and space, saving the world from Shredder, Krang, and their minions.

In *High School*, entering the Code during the eleventh-grade history class level gives you extra physical and psychological endurance scores equivalent to +25 resistance versus bullying. This bonus unlocks new dialogue options, so that when the kid behind you keeps poking you relentlessly in the back while chanting "Hey Limpy, hey Limpy, hey Limpy," you can select "Quietly endure it" in addition to the previously available "Scream FUCK OFF and get kicked out of class," "Turn around and punch him in the face and get suspended," and "Turn around and stab him in the throat with your pen and get expelled" options.

In *The Legendary Bar & Eatery*, entering the Code grants you and your entire party +5 resistance to alcohol. This bonus makes the driving minigame at the end of the level trivially easy to beat and is the only way to complete the game with Aerith remaining in your party.

In *Tetris* for the NES, you may pause the game once per level and enter the Code to transform the current game piece (n.b. those things are called *tetrominoes*! Isn't that *adorable*?) into the always-useful I-shaped one.

In *Your Shitty Job*, entering the Code at any point triggers the Ask for a Raise event. After this seemingly interminable cutscene plays, all defeated enemies will have a ten percent higher drop rate for treasure for the remainder of the game.

In *Social Situations*, enter the Code immediately before walking through the front door. The resulting +2 Constitution bonus will let you shrug off the Panic Attack status effect, making you temporarily invulnerable. The only way to beat the level without this bonus is to have Too Much Whiskey and/or Klonopin equipped.

In *Your Last Relationship*, enter the Code at any point before the eighteen-month anniversary level. You will be granted ninety-nine lives and ninety-nine continues, so you can keep on fucking everything up again and again and again.

In *Tiny Toon Adventures: Wacky Sports Challenge* for the SNES, if the Code is entered at the title screen, a level-select feature becomes available.

Invasion Games

WHEN VIDEO ARCADES WERE STILL A THING, THIS WAS *THE ONE*, a transcendent world to crawl into and get lost in. Unsurpassed and, since the rise to ubiquity of home consoles, probably now unsurpassable. Video Invasion, at 3500 Bathurst Street, halfway between avenues Wilson and Lawrence, hosted some of the most glorious, most tinnitus-inducing birthday parties that a twelve-year-old North Yorker could ever hope for. Inside, its atmosphere bulged with screams of virtual triumph and of digital mortality, incense of pizza grease, and clinks and bleeps of coin-operated spacecraft piloted by highly caffeinated preteens. You know, the way God intended.

This was where, over the course of a single afternoon, you'd spend like sixty bucks of your parents' hard-earned money in tokens to beat *Turtles in Time* with three other kids from Hebrew school; where you'd perfect your machine gunning skills on the *Terminator 2* cabinet (although you were still too young to have seen *Terminator 2*); where you'd learn to fly everything from a blimp to a UFO in *Time Pilot*. There were kind of a lot of time travel-themed games, come to think of it. Oh, also there was an actual functioning time machine. That was probably a coincidence.

If you were the birthday boy or girl, inevitably at some point during the celebration, usually after cake but before vomiting from eating too much cake (or from eating the plastic cake decorations that were not really edible but just looked *so delicious* that you couldn't help yourself—and actually *were* pretty tasty so, you know, no regrets), an arcade employee would come find you and ask you a question.

This man or woman was about your age—your age *now*, as you

read this. On his or her face lived a look of exhausted exhilaration, as if having this much fun *as a job* was just barely bearable. The employee wore an apron with the arcade's laughing, bowling-pin-shaped clown mascot embroidered on its front. You could be forgiven for assuming at first that this employee was *in the family way*, but no, rather it was the *apron*, a garment composed entirely of sewn-together pockets, that was itself pregnant with *tokens*—the arcade's own minted scrip, gold-coloured coins costing one-third of a dollar that you had to use for the games in lieu of cash. And so with each step the employee took, a clanging carillon radiated in every direction, the tokens' sound drawing children into the employee's gravity like some postmodern Pied Piper. You know that story? Yeah, it was a lot like that.

The question, the question that this jangling, animated employee asked you on your birthday, was this: *Do you want to see the time machine?*

So you went to see the time machine. Because of course you did.

Shown to a back room, not hidden but with *PRIVATE* stickered across its door at adult-height and cordoned off with red velvet rope that might as well have been a force field for its obstructive effect. The employee moved that rope aside like it was nothing, opened the door for you, and you entered. With the door closed again behind you, the arcade's chaos vanished; this room was silent. Inside: time machine, just as promised, resembling precisely the one from that H.G. Wells novel you read last summer—a clockwork affair, not a car but more of a treadmill inside a pair of shining rings, each maybe seven feet in diameter, interlocked with one another at ninety-degree angles. All nickel and ivory and quartz and dials and levers. Below the control panel, a coin acceptor reading *INSERT SIX TOKENS*. Most expensive machine in the whole damn place, but you got inside and did what it said.

And it worked.

Around you, hours and then years flew forward. Walls all turned clear, and you could see through the room, through the building, through the world. From your privileged point there on Bathurst Street, you watched history run ahead as if there were a prize for the first person to get to the end of it. That person was you, and the end was today. Today, the day that you read this. Because it was your birthday, you got to see it with your own two eyes. The invasion. The video invasion.

What you always believed was the image of a clown in the shape of a sort of flattened lemniscate, you now learned was in fact the transgression into our world of something the human eye and mind could never truly comprehend. They were everywhere, *everywhere*—in every building, every room, in every hidden corner, just on the other side of every surface. Behind the bookcase. Under the fridge. Where did they come from? What, if anything, did they want? You didn't know. You'd never know.

As fast as it forwarded, history then reversed, and you returned to your birthday party with information but not understanding. Played some *Time Soldiers*. Vomited cake.

What you saw that day never left you, and nobody who hadn't celebrated a birthday there even believed it when you told them. Who could blame them? But everyone who had, did. It wasn't a dream. All the accounts matched up.

Of course, today has arrived and clearly there's been no invasion. Not in any way you can perceive. Just look around you. The arcade's not even there anymore. What was it that you saw that day? A warning? A promise? An image of what would be or of what could be? It's impossible to know. Everything about that place is gone now except its memory and maybe, at the bottom of some forgotten drawer somewhere, in a house in which you no longer live, a gold-coloured coin or two. The only sign remaining that once you were young. You're *sure* that you were. You must have been.

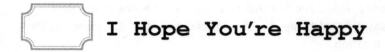

I Hope You're Happy

You ruined typewriters for me.

Used Miracles

WHEN THE DOORS FINALLY OPEN AND YOU STEP—*STUMBLE* IS MORE like it—off the subway car, the last train of the night, the one that you were so grateful to catch, that saved you from having to take the dreaded twenty-four hour bus (affectionately nicknamed the "Vomit Comet" by those unfortunate enough to require its services) or spending upwards of fifty dollars on a taxi, there, standing on the otherwise barren platform, two very tall men dressed identically in white trousers and white jackets are waiting for you.

Objective

To obtain a full-time position with an organization where I can learn and expand my abilities while at the same time utilizing my talent and experience to contribute to the well-being of the world at large in a positive, meaningful way.

"Can I help you?" You're trying not to be rude. Maybe this is all just some small misunderstanding. But really, the two of them have their hands on you in a very deliberate way. You don't appreciate it. Each of them holds you, with one hand, by one of your shoulders. You couldn't break away or escape if you tried. The pressure with which their fingers grip you isn't painful, but it's solid. Serious. "I'm drunk," you say, "but I'm not that drunk." You say, "I'm not going to fall over or anything. I don't need you to hold me up. But, uh, thanks anyway."

When you look up at one of them, he looks back down at you. His face is blank. Without malice. Without anything. He stays quiet. You look up at the other one.

"We're here to apprehend you," that one says. Smooth. Calm. Official. "We're taking you into our custody."

Somehow this does not comfort you.

"Oh," you say. "Are you—are you police officers?"

The two men look like they could be twins, maybe. Fraternal twins, though, not identical. Their clothes fit perfectly. Their skin is naturally golden, smooth, as if they spend all their vacation time on a beach somewhere and genuinely forget their troubles while there. This is no ultraviolet sarcophagus sort of tan. Not one hair or follicle is visible on either of their faces. Both of them could probably use a bit of a haircut soon.

"No," the one says. "We are not police officers."

Education and Experience

I attended Such-and-Such Secondary School, graduating with honours.

For the next eleven years, I worked at the ---------- Automotive Manufacturing Plant in -------, until several months ago, when it was closed and all three thousand people employed there were laid off.

I don't and can't blame the corporation for closing the plant. These are difficult times. The world economy is unpredictable to say the least, and those who are attempting to predict it foresee nothing but trouble ahead. Naturally, people are tightening their belts. Many simply can't afford the luxury of a new car these days—and the ones who would be willing to risk it are having difficulty convincing any bank to give them a loan in these tumultuous circumstances. Again, who can blame them? Compounding the problem, those who can easily afford a new vehicle are trending away from the sort of conveyances that we produce(d) at the plant. They're buying hybrids or, at best, the smallest and most fuel-efficient gasoline-powered cars they can find. Nobody wants a giant thing that takes up two full lanes of traffic and gets one mile to the gallon anymore. Why would they? It's just not efficient in a financial or environmental sense.

All right, I suppose I do blame the company in the sense that they could have predicted this downturn in the demand for their products and adjusted their business model accordingly. If they had been making the cars that people wanted to buy, or at least had been managing their business in a responsible way, maybe none of this would be happening. Then again, maybe it would be anyway. What it comes down to, ultimately, is that they are running a business and not a charity. They don't owe me a job; on the contrary, I considered myself overwhelmingly fortunate to have retained my position for as long as I did, and I was always more than fairly recompensed, with ample vacation time and countless benefits. No, I just can't hold these layoffs against them. For all my faults and shortcomings, I am not that ungrateful a person.

"Are you going to kill me?" you say, with intoxicated calm. You say, "Don't kill me, okay? I can't die yet. There's a war going on, and I want to see who wins."

They take you to a car—a white car, a large sedan—parked outside in the subway station's lot. They got a good spot, too, right by the entrance. Of course it's two in the morning, so the place is empty and deserted aside from this one car. But still. You have to pay to park here. These guys aren't fooling around.

Still holding you by a shoulder each, one of them—the one who hasn't spoken yet—opens the rear door of the car and gestures that you should get in. You get in. Because, what the hell, what are you going to do, run? They could easily catch you, particularly since in your current state you'd probably succeed only in staggering about five feet, if you're lucky, before pitching over and vomiting onto the pavement.

The door closes, and then the two men get into the front seats. The inside of the car is upholstered in leather. Black. It's cold even through your clothes, and you kind of slide around a little.

From the driver's seat, one of the men, the one who talks, says, "We're not going to kill you." Then, as if to reinforce the point, he says, "Put on your seatbelt."

You put on your seatbelt.

The engine starts and the car pulls out of the lot then goes down the street. Outside it's dark, obviously, and you're pretty intoxicated anyway, so you can't keep track of exactly where you're being taken, but the two men in the front haven't tried to blindfold you or otherwise attempt to obscure your vision, so they must not, you reason, be too concerned about your seeing where you're going. Should that scare you or not? Idly, you gaze out the window, then at the backs of the men's heads for a while. You massage the seat beside you, enjoying the temperature and texture of the leather. You look out the window some more.

"We saw," says the man driving, apropos of nothing, after minutes and minutes of silence, "your resume. Well, our ... our *boss* saw it. Our *superior*. You posted it on that website. He liked it. It showed creativity. And loyalty. We were sent to retrieve you."

This is not something you expected.

"Wait," you say. "So you mean this is about a job, you have a job for me?"

"There is ... " and the driver trails off here for a second, trying to come up with the right phrasing. Finally he decides on: "There's a position that has become available."

"What is it?" you ask. "What would I have to do?"

"Whatever seems necessary at the time."

"How much does it pay?"

"You'll be compensated in accordance with what you earn."

Even as drunk as you are, you know these are not useful responses. Now you're starting to wonder if these guys are with the mob or something. But what could they possibly want *you* for? And how did they know where to find you, anyway? Nobody had known where you were tonight; you didn't want anyone to know, so you hadn't told anyone. These two couldn't have just been trailing you, because they were waiting for you at the subway station when you disembarked. Was there someone else, following you around, reporting your location and movements to these two, so they could be there to accost you? What would be the point of that? Who are you to them, anyway? You're nobody.

You squeeze your eyes shut tight, push them in with your fingers until white fireworks of geometric shapes explode in the darkness.

"Are you all right?" the driver says. He sounds genuine but not overly concerned.

"I've got a headache," you say. You open your eyes again, and the world slowly drains back into your awareness. "Just a bit of a headache. That's all."

With confidence and authority, the man declares: "You're dehydrated. You ought to be drinking more water."

That's true, you think. You say so. You say, "That's true," and then you lean back, sliding down in the large back seat of the car, take a few deep breaths, and imagine that you're preparing for an important presentation.

Skills and Interests

I was in a play once. I didn't, and don't, consider myself an actor. But I was sort of in love with the director—well, maybe "in love" is too strong; it was high school, I had a crush on the director of the play—and allowed myself to be convinced to audition, and I got a part. Not the lead or anything, but I wasn't playing "Tree #2" either. I had a few lines. More than a few. I could probably still remember them if I tried.

The point is that I was in this play and I learned something about myself from the experience. Probably I wasn't any good, but what I realized was that even though I was scared to death of standing up there on the stage and performing in front of all those people, once I actually got up there, all my fear and anxiety melted away, and I was perfectly calm as I recited my lines. It didn't hurt that the lights were so bright I couldn't see anything, so I wasn't even sure that there was anyone out there in the audience.

When I was up there, I knew exactly what I had to do. There were these lines that had been written for me, I knew what they were, and all I had to do was say them. There were stage directions, and I was required only to follow them. And when my part was done, it was done. There was room for interpretation—plenty of room for it, as a matter of fact; the director was very open to that sort of thing—but ultimately I had my instructions, and my only concern was carrying them out correctly. When I compared that to the way I felt every other day in every other situation—how my every word and action made me feel like I was trying to extract the one black marble from a bowl full of white ones, trying to do the right thing but not knowing how or even what that right thing was, or even if there was a right thing at all—I felt so much better. So much more free. Once I had made the decision to participate, it was the strict limitations of the script that in the end gave me freedom. And freedom gave me peace.

I'm good at following instructions, I guess, is the point.

When you pull up beside this building, large and square and white and grey, that looks like it's made out of Lego™—like you could take it apart and put it back together as anything you wanted it to be: a museum, a fire station, a library, a bank, a house of prayer—you stop. That is, the car stops, and you are inside the car, so you stop too, though it wasn't particularly your intention to end up here. But it seems as if this is the destination of the two men who have, you might as well admit it, kidnapped you. And so you assume that it is the office of their employer, whoever that is, the one who is interested in possibly acquiring your services. For what? You're reluctant to press for that answer any more than you have already. Pretty much you feel as if you'd better not look a gift horse in the mouth. If there's an opportunity here, you think you really should go for it. You have expenses, after all. There's credit card bills, cellphone bills. Winter is coming, heat is expensive. You've got a family to feed, maybe. Beggars can't, in most circumstances, you reason, be choosers.

The engine shuts off and the two men open the front doors and get out of the car. You take off your seatbelt, open your own door, and exit as well. One of the men gestures with his chin at the front door of the building. They don't take hold of you this time, but only begin to walk at a very comfortable pace toward the place ahead of you. You follow them, looking not at the building itself but instead at the back of the legs of the two men's white trousers.

Trousers. Why did you think *trousers*? Who says *trousers*? They're pants. You've never thought the word trousers before in your entire life. But for some reason, describing these men as wearing mere pants seems insufficiently serious. So: trousers.

You know now that you must be scared, because instead of thinking about why you're here or what you're going to do when you get inside the place you're being guided to, you're thinking about the difference between pants and trousers.

Now you've reached the door. The two men in front of you part and move to either side of the threshold. Clearing the way for you. No one, you suddenly understand, is going to force you anymore.

You open the door. You go in.

Flight Risk

"EXCUSE ME, SIR."

I looked up from the bag of honey-roasted peanuts, one of which I had already removed and was holding in my left hand as it slowly stained my fingertips the yellowish-brown of peanut oil and artificial honey-roasting agents. I was in the aisle seat. That was always my first choice because I'd noticed that I seemed to go to the bathroom more than most other people—from boredom and restlessness more than any real urological necessity—and it was a lot less annoying to have someone step over me once or twice during the flight than it would be to have to step over someone else a dozen times in the same period. Not only is it extremely irritating for everyone involved, but if you get up to go to the bathroom more than, say, five times, your neighbour always starts looking at you funny, like she's trying to figure out whether you're really doing drugs or masturbating back there or if you just have serious bladder issues and might treat her to an impromptu golden shower if she doesn't get out of your way fast enough. It's just easier on the aisle. Besides, they mostly close the window-shade for over half the flight anyway, and how long can you really look at the top of a cloud before you get tired of it? Yeah, okay, you're white and fluffy. Very nice. I get it. Can we move on now?

The stewardess (or what are we supposed to call them now, Flight Hostess? Sky Wench? Whatever) was pretty—stewardess-pretty, which is to say, pretty in a creepy, almost robotic, uncanny valley sort of way—dressed in the clean, no-nonsense colour of the airline, which was blue or grey or possibly dark green; it was hard to tell. Her face wore an expression like there was a termite infestation in the stick up her ass.

124

"Is there something wrong, sir?" she asked.

"Uh, no. Why would there be something wrong?"

"I just happened to notice that you seemed to be ... muttering."

"Muttering?"

"Yes. Muttering."

"Muttering."

Had I been? Muttering? *Muttering*. What a stupid word.

"And I just wanted to make sure that you weren't ... you know ... that there wasn't anything wrong."

"I'm not sure I understand what you mean," I said.

"Well, you see, sir, this is ... a rather sensitive topic." She was speaking in the most circumspect way possible, sentences spinning around and around the point so that I might not notice if, at the end of it, she turned out to be accusing me of something. "You've just opened your *complimentary* bag of peanuts, and it looked as if you were about to eat one—" She gestured to my left hand, which by now was being eroded by the peanut grease; I would be lucky if I still had five fingerprints left by the time I managed to get the thing into my mouth. "And then your lips started moving, and I wanted to make certain that you weren't ... well, *you know*."

"Um, I *don't* know, I'm afraid. You'll have to be a little more specific."

She frowned. It didn't become her. I'd still have hit that, though.

"I wanted to make certain that you weren't ..." She said something under her breath. *Muttered* something. I couldn't hear.

"I'm sorry? I didn't catch that last part."

"*Praying*," she hissed, evidently furious that I had forced her to utter such an obscenity. "I wanted to make sure that you were not *praying*. We've been known to have people *say blessings* on their in-flight food on occasion, and on this airline, as I'm sure you are aware, we have a zero-tolerance policy on such behaviour."

I blinked several times. I put the corrosively anointed peanut carefully back into the bag whence it came.

"I'm sorry, but did you just say that *praying* is not permitted on this airline?"

"Don't act like this is new information to you, sir," she condescended. "In this *Post-Nine-Eleven World*, we can't be too careful, now, can we?"

I was pretty sure that we *could* be, and in fact were being too careful, as a matter of fact. Also, I was fairly certain that I would have been shot with a Taser if I had been the one to say those numbers aloud rather than the stewardess.

"I was not aware of this policy," I said, treading lightly.

"I find that difficult to believe, sir."

"You find that difficult to believe."

"That's right."

"And what *do* you believe, then, exactly?"

"I believe—" she began, then stopped herself, with a terrified look on her face as if she were afraid someone might have heard her. "I mean, I don't believe anything. I only meant that I ... I *suspected* that you may have been ..."

By that point I had had enough of this nonsense.

"Look, could you leave me alone, please? I'm trying to relax here. I'll call you if I need my pillow fluffed."

"Do not take that attitude with me, sir!"

"I'm not taking any attitude with you, I just—"

"I am a highly trained professional, and if you think that we are not serious about our policies, I will have you know that just today we successfully prevented both a woman wearing a crucifix and a man with a *beard* from boarding this very flight. Not the good kind of beard, this was not a secular beard, I assure you. And earlier in the week, police were dispatched to the home of one person who tried to order a kosher meal."

"I certainly salute you for your vigilance, and I'm sure you'll be awarded the purple heart for it as soon as we land, but I'm just trying to—"

"There is no need to become hostile, sir."

"I am not becoming hostile!" I said, hostilely.

"Sir, I insist that you calm down, or I'm afraid we will be forced to remove you from this flight."

"Remove me from the flight! I didn't *do* anything. I was just trying to eat some peanuts, for God's sake!"

The stewardess's eyes flashed. With one mechanical motion she raised her wrist to her mouth, and spoke into what seemed to be some kind of walkie-talkie device affixed to her watch.

"*G-Word* detected in seat 36-D," she said. "We have a Believer on board. Repeat: we have a Believer on board."

Instantly, I felt the seatbelt tighten painfully around my waist. Leather restraints emerged from the armrests, as well as from under my seat, gripping my arms and legs so that I couldn't budge an inch in any direction. The bag of peanuts fell from my hand and dropped to the floor, spilling delicious-looking synthetic legumes everywhere. What a waste. Another restraint swung around from the headrest behind me, over my mouth. I was trapped, completely immobilized.

I struggled against the straps; I tried to scream, but it was no use. All throughout the fuselage, other passengers were turning to see what all the commotion was about, simultaneously terrified and enraptured. Muttering to each other, all muttering.

A voice of unquestionable authority issued forth from above.

"Attention all passengers," it said, "this is your captain speaking. Due to a potential flight risk on board, we will be unable to proceed to our destination. For your safety, we are going to be forced to reverse course and return to Winnipeg. Please stay calm and remain in your seats. We apologize for the inconvenience."

A collective groan emerged from everyone on board but me. My eyes—the only parts of me that I could still move—darted desperately back and forth. Out the window, all I could see was clouds.

 # Death

God, if it can happen to *David Bowie*, it could happen to *anybody*.

If you're reading this, I am alive.

IF YOU DON'T STOP DRINKING, YOU ARE GOING TO DIE.

If I had started taking the medicine when I should have, when I first understood that I really had a problem—thirteen years earlier or ten or two, or even if I'd started taking the medicine just one year earlier—who knows what I could have accomplished, what wouldn't have seemed too scary or too impossible, what I would have created instead of hiding away under the covers waiting for the monsters like I did. If you wait long enough, the monsters always come.

If wishes were horses—how does that thing go again? If wishes were horses, then beggars would ride, is that right?

If the sun went out right now, it would take eight minutes before anyone here on earth even noticed, and by then it would be way too late to do anything about it. If the dinosaurs hadn't died out, do you think they would have evolved into sentient beings like us, with language and art and religion and war? If an asteroid like that were to strike again today, we'd end up just like them. If we start sending colonists to Mars as soon as technologically possible, do you think we could save ourselves? If the dinosaurs had stuck around, would *they* have gone to Mars, do you think?

If I'd lied instead of telling the truth ... do me a favour: next time, remind me to lie.

If you hadn't been so hung over, I guarantee that you would have done great that day. If your parents had known how to show you love, none of this stupid needless bullshit ever would have happened; you would be happy and healthy and successful right now instead of vomiting down the front of your dress twenty minutes after last call.

If God exists, He's going to have a lot of explaining to do ...

and I'm going to have a lot of apologizing to do, so I guess we're probably even.

If we start a band, it should be called Laura Palmer's Boobs. If you listen very carefully, you'll hear somebody whispering goodnight to their children at seven minutes and fifty-six seconds into the final track on the debut album.

If only you hadn't answered that call, you know? If only you hadn't sent that text. If only you hadn't gone over there that night. If only you'd stuck to your guns.

If you write one page per day, by the end of the year you'll have a novel. If readers will forgive a little gimmick here and there, I have a pretty good idea for one, I think. If I am ever unable to make my own medical decisions, listen, I don't want to "die with dignity," okay, promise you will make those doctors plug me into every machine they can find—respirator, dialysis, that heart machine thing, air conditioner, PlayStation, vacuum cleaner, George Foreman Grill, everything, all of it, those are my wishes, and I expect you to honour them. If I die before I have the chance to do it myself, please burn all my journals and papers, my hard drives and DVD-Rs—that is what I would have wanted.

If I get on the 12:30 bus, I can be there by 6:45—will you meet me at the station?

If you want to get to her, you'll have to go through me first. If you think that just because I'm old and short and not very athletic and don't have any tattoos, I'll just let you ruin the lives of people I love without even putting up a fight, you are very, very mistaken, my friend. If you've never heard the sound of a human being's skull cracking against the corner of an oak table snowy with powdered morphine, then I can pretty much guarantee you're not going to like hearing your own. If you call the police, make sure you tell them how we got here—and remember that I've got the whole conversation saved on my phone at home, and in the cloud. If you think I'm bluffing, just try me.

If you mix the medicine into orange juice, you can hardly taste it at all.

If you're looking for sympathy, with your paranoid conspiracy theories, your persecution complex, your thought-terminating clichés, and your hundreds of Twitter followers—well, if that's what you want from me, sorry but you are not going to get it, you just aren't.

If I didn't know any better, I'd think that you were trying to hide something.

If I can just finish this one level, if I can beat this one boss, if I can get to the next save point, if I can jump to that ledge over there, if the goddamn computer ever stops cheating, then yes, I can turn this off and come back to bed. If that's the right time showing on the clock, then the sun will be coming up soon anyway, so I might as well ... If that's really how you feel about it, then fine.

If they kill off Tyrion or Arya, I'm out, I swear to God.

If I don't find a job soon, I'm going to kill myself. If I'd listened to everybody and gone to law school, I wouldn't be living in this rat hole, eating ramen four days a week and hot dogs the other three. If I got my license, I could drive an Uber, I guess, how hard could that be? If I had the money, I would get so much plastic surgery, I'm not even kidding. If I start making coffee at home, I could save like five hundred dollars a year, but what would I do all day if I didn't go to Starbucks? If I get that grant from the Council, everything will be okay. If the other guy had won, we wouldn't be in this mess right now—we'd be in some completely different mess and complaining about that instead. If we gave every citizen a guaranteed minimum income of $20,000 a year—and, look, you know my politics; I'm not one of those utopian, probiotic, anti-GMO, Chomsky-sucking juice cleanse people, just hear me out—if we did that, it would actually be way cheaper than our current welfare system, I mean, just do the math.

If *ifs* and *buts* were candy and nuts, we'd all have a *freilichen Purim*.

If I had superpowers, I would be a hero. If you want to laugh, then laugh, but I would. If I could get out of bed a little earlier in the morning, I could really get some stuff done. If I could think of anything to do, that is. If I made a list, a plan, a schedule. If I started with a big, leisurely breakfast—toast and eggs and pancakes and hash browns and fruit salad and yogurt and maybe a muffin, blueberry or something, or banana nut, that's a good muffin, and a big mug of tea with lots of lemon, while listening to Mozart or AC/DC to really get my blood marching—I'd have the energy to go all day. If I got up before dawn, I could go for a run and watch the sun rise. If I had the right shoes for it. If I went to bed earlier, I could wake up earlier. If it didn't take me so long to fall asleep at night. If I put away the laptop and the iPhone and the 3DS a little sooner, maybe. If I didn't eat dinner so late. If I weren't so sad all the time, I wouldn't be so tired all the time, I bet. If I could get myself to shower and brush my teeth twice a day every single day, that would probably help a lot. If I hadn't been so ugly as a child, I'd have grown up much happier.

If you see him again, ever, no matter what, it's over.

Concentrate Here for 294 Seconds

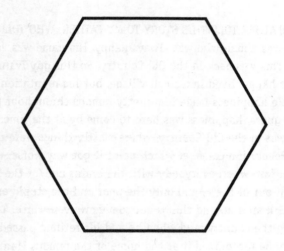

The Very Last Story Ever

No
epigraph.
Too
obvious/
cliché.
AUTHOR

MY GRANDFATHER TOLD THIS STORY TO MY FATHER, WHO TOLD IT TO ME.
There was a man who was always happy. His name was, let's
say, Ivan. This was back in the Old Country. So this guy Ivan, who
was always happy, lived in a small village, but his reputation for
unshakeable happiness made him pretty famous throughout the land.
Because, I guess, happiness was hard to come by at the time. ~~Like I~~
~~said, this was in the Old Country, where mostly things were real shitty,~~
~~until the Revolution came, at which point it got way worse, until~~
~~the Dissolution, when everybody with the brains and/or the means~~

Cut all
this.
Nobody
cares
about
your dumb
retro-
gressive
politics.
AUTHOR

~~got the hell out of there, and only the poor and the stupid and the~~
~~corrupt stuck around, and things got somehow even worse.~~ The Czar
was touring the country, and when he and his retinue passed through
this village, he recognized it as the home of the famous Man Who Was
Always Happy. The Czar had everything that he'd ever wanted, and if
he thought of something that he didn't have, his toadies would have
it brought to him within the hour. He still wasn't happy. That some
dirt-eating peasant could be happy all the time while he, the Czar, sat
surrounded day after day by sumptuous foods, radiant treasures, and
beautiful women and yet was still miserable ... well, it rankled. ~~You~~
~~know the type.~~

The Czar ordered his retinue to stop in this village. The retinue
stopped. The Czar commanded, "Bring to me the man who is always
happy—if he really exists." Within the hour, Ivan was found and
brought out before the Czar.

All those dirt-eating peasants crowded around to watch as the
Czar spoke to Ivan in the village square. All of the Czar's retainers
wondered what the mighty Czar could possibly have to say to this

nobody. Ivan stood up straight, lowered his eyes to a respectful level, and smiled.

The Czar said, "I've heard about you. You're the man who's always happy. Even as far as the Winter Palace we've heard about you."

Ivan said, "I'm honoured, Your Imperial Majesty." He had to look up the correct form of address for the Czar before leaving the house, but he was happy to do it. He liked learning new things.

"It doesn't seem possible for any person to be happy *all the time*," the Czar said. He didn't mention how difficult it was, when in his blackest moods, even to remember what happiness was like or to imagine ever feeling happy again in the future.

"I know it's very unusual," Ivan said, "but it's true—I'm just naturally happy. Nothing so terrible has ever happened in my life to ruin my good mood. Even as a baby, I never cried. I've been blessed with the gift of happiness."

The Czar said, "We'll see about that. Tonight at midnight, you'll return here to the village square. I will be waiting, and I will ask you three questions. I'll even give you the questions in advance right now, so you can think them over. Question one: how many grains of sand are there on the beach? Question two: how many stars are there in the sky? Question three: what will I be thinking at that moment when we meet again? If you don't answer all three questions correctly, you'll be hanged in the morning. See you at midnight. I'll be interested to see how happy you are then."

The Czar returned to his litter, attended by his retinue, and the villagers assembled around were a woeful whirl of whispers. On Ivan's face appeared an expression that no one had ever seen there before. For the first time in his life, he was upset. Terrified. *Unhappy.*

Soon the crowd dispersed. Almost worse than the death sentence the Czar had pronounced was the fact that it had succeeded in breaking Ivan's contentment. No one knew what to do. No one knew what to say. So, like most people do at times like this, they disappeared.

Except for one person. Ivan's friend, a Jew. ~~The clever guy in these stories is always a Jew.~~

His friend put a hand on Ivan's shoulder. "Don't worry," he said. "Everything will be fine."

"How will everything be fine?" Ivan said, surprised to hear in his own voice that aggressive, omnidirectional scorn that he now understood to be a peculiar mix of terror and doubt. "You heard the Czar! He'll be coming back at midnight. I can't possibly give the right answers to his questions. I'm as good as dead."

Ivan's friend was not deterred. "When the Czar returns, I'll go in your place. It will be dark, and I'll put on your clothes, and I'll answer his questions instead of you."

"Then he'll just kill you instead of me!" Ivan said. "Or, if he discovers that we're trying to trick him, he'll have both of us killed. No, I appreciate what you're trying to do for me, but it's hopeless."

"I insist on this," Ivan's friend said. "I'll go in your place, and neither one of us will die. I promise."

"I don't know what you have planned," Ivan said, "but if you're sure, then I trust you. Thank you, and good luck."

At midnight, as promised, the Czar and his retinue returned to the village square. The villagers came back too—nothing like this had ever happened here as long as any of them had lived. Ivan's friend, dressed in Ivan's clothes, made straight for the Czar. He wore a hooded cloak so his face was in shadow; there were no lights, and the sky was cloudy. The Czar began to speak.

"First question," he said. "How many grains of sand are there on the beach?"

Ivan's friend had his answers prepared. "There are a hundred billion grains of sand on the beach," he said. "If you don't believe me, you're free to count them yourself."

Nobody had expected that response—or any response, really. Least of all the Czar.

"I have to admit you've got me there," the Czar replied. He sounded impressed. "Second question: how many stars are there in the sky?" By this point, the Czar had a pretty good idea what Ivan's answer was going to be.

"There are two hundred billion billion stars in the sky," Ivan's friend said. "And if you don't believe me—"

"I'm free to count them myself, yes. This last one won't be as simple, smart guy. Third question: what am I thinking right now?"

"What you're thinking is that you're speaking right now to Ivan, the man who is always happy." The man pulled the hood away from his head and now, even in the dark, it was obvious that this wasn't Ivan at all, but instead his friend the Jew, gone in his place. "But you aren't."

That's it. That's the story. Cute, right? There's probably a moral in there somewhere, but I'm not exactly sure what it's supposed to be. The guy saved his friend's life, but the Czar still actually did manage to wreck Ivan's perfect happiness. We don't get to know what happened to any of them after the end of the story: how they lived or how they changed, what the event meant to them or how it affected the way that they raised their families and passed down their traditions to the next generation or any of that stuff. Which is important, that stuff.

So here's another story. My grandfather also told it to my father, who told it to me.

This one's true.

Where my dad's parents were from, geopolitically the whole region was a complete mess for the entire twentieth century. For hundreds of years it had been part of the Austrian Empire (simple enough), until the Revolution of 1848 created a new sovereign Hungary. After the First World War, the place became part of Czechoslovakia but then was re-annexed by Hungary in 1939~~, on March 16, forty years before I was born, to the day, which is a little weird I guess, but the chances of the dates coinciding are only one in three hundred and sixty-five, after all, which isn't that astronomically unlikely.~~ Then the Nazis invaded, but soon after, the place was captured by the Ukrainian Red Army, ~~which sounds like a good thing, right? Getting it away from the Nazis? Except that the Ukrainians were somehow even worse. What the Nazis didn't have the stomach to do to the Jews, the Ukrainians lined up to volunteer for. Nice people.~~ Anyway, it became part of the USSR until the collapse of the Soviet Union. Now it's part of Ukraine, officially.

During the war, my grandfather was in a Nazi slave labour camp. He'd been drafted into the army by the Czechoslovakians, then captured as a POW by the Germans and put to work. The prisoners were mostly Jews, but this wasn't a concentration camp. My grandmother was taken to the famous Auschwitz concentration camp in Poland, as was my grandfather's daughter from his first marriage—that's my father's half-sister. On my grandmother's side, besides her, nobody came out. So this slave labour camp wasn't an extermination camp, but they certainly didn't try very hard to keep people alive there.

He was a strong guy, my grandfather, which was lucky, because in the labour camps, if you weren't strong, you were definitely dead. You could be strong *and* dead, sometimes, but you couldn't be weak and alive. Not for very long. People starved. People got sick or got injured—either from the work itself or beatings from the guards for not working hard enough. And if you were too hungry or sick or injured to work, they shot you.

One night—when I imagine it, it's cold, you can see your breath, and there's a full, white moon in the sky—my grandfather was returning to the barracks when he saw the commandant of the camp on his way to the outhouse. Now this guy, the commandant, was a real bastard, even for a Nazi. While none of the camps were exactly a picnic, the tenor of each depended a lot on the personality of the guy in charge, and this one was bad. Maybe not the worst; definitely not the best. My grandfather had seen other prisoners beaten and starved and shot on this man's orders.

The commandant entered the outhouse. My grandfather approached it and waited just outside. Maybe he held his breath. How could his blood not have rumbled like thunder? And when the commandant finished and creaked the door open, my grandfather struck: pushed him back inside, shut the door behind them, and started to pound this Nazi in the gut. Like I said, my grandfather was a strong guy; even the guards were afraid of him—their cruelty was often a little muted when he was around. Not tall but broad, hard as a cast-iron stove and muscled from work, work like I'll never see in my life. Envision this tough-ass Jew, this Samson in his chains, think of the power in his righteous rage; picture his captor, this Philistine in Hugo Boss, this beatified goon who crushed the lives of thousands, cowering on the latrine as he's pummelled by some degenerate *untermensch*.

My grandfather pounded this Nazi in the stomach as hard as he could for as long as he thought he could without getting caught, then left him there in the outhouse and went back to barracks. The next morning, the guards announced that the commandant was very sick. The day after that, they announced that he was dead. Someone else was soon brought in to replace him, of course. But so what? Like it says in Proverbs: *when evil people perish, there is joy*.

Plenty of details are missing—I know this was late in the war, but not the specific year; I don't know the name of the camp or of the commandant. My father was reluctant to pry any deeper than my grandfather was willing to tell, which is understandable, but which both he and I regret. But this happened. This was a thing that happened in the world.

When these events occurred, my grandfather was younger than I am now. I still feel like a dumb little kid, but he had already lost his entire family—parents, siblings, wife, all but one of his children; after the war, not only did he survive, but he built a *new* family, suffered under Stalin and then under Khrushchev, escaped the Soviet Union (a whole other story of its own), and started a new life not once but twice—first in Israel, then Canada—got a shitty job at a junkyard by day and another as night janitor at city hall, and somehow made enough to support my grandmother (who also worked, cleaning houses) and my father, to put food on the table and buy a nice house with cherry trees in the yard and plastic over the furniture. My family and I still avail of the fruits of the torture and slavery that my grandfather was forced to endure. He's gone—almost his whole generation is gone—but his pain will outlive us all.

Compared to the world in which my grandparents were born, the world I live in is practically messianic. I've never had to hide in an attic or pretend to be somebody I'm not or say anything that I don't believe. I've never missed a meal or had to sleep in the cold. There is even a place out there—can you imagine?—that promises to take me when this rich and comfortable nation finally kicks us all out, like they all eventually do, no matter how nice they are to your face.

But am I happy? Of course I'm not happy. I have to take pills just so I don't want to die all the time. Not that I'm not grateful for those pills. But this is what my grandparents suffered and died for? So that I could sleep until noon in my huge, warm bed and spend all day reading books and playing games and telling stories? So that I could sit here *pushing fucking buttons*? How is that fair? Since the day I was born, I've been carried on silk pillows by hundreds of centuries of other people's suffering. My feet have never touched the ground. Not only are there no numbers on my arms, there aren't even callouses on my fingers. I'm not asking for things to be harder. God forbid. But how can I ever look the past in the eye? How do I have the nerve to exist at all with the awareness of everything that led to me being here? What gives me the right to live inside this flesh-carved fallout shelter of history? Is there any way I can possibly make it all have been worth it? These are not rhetorical questions. I really need to know. Tell me. *What am I supposed to do?*

Acknowledgements

Thanks to: The Precondition for the Possibility of Experience; my parents; Hal Niedzviecki; Danila Botha; Karen Correia da Silva; Curran Folkers; Sarah Beaudin; Maddy Curry; Daniel Sinker; Emily Schultz; Bryan Jay Ibeas; Elizabeth Rodriguez; Emma Healey; Robert J. Sawyer; Karl Schroeder; Jennifer Murray, Holly Kent, and everyone at the Ontario Book Publishers Organization; Kaile H. Glick; Taranjeet Kaur Brar; Jim Nason, Heather Wood, Deanna Janovski, and everyone at Tightrope Books; and the crew at Overthinking It.

About the Author

PHOTO: Arezou Firouzeh

Richard Rosenbaum is the author of the novel *Pretend to Feel* (Now Or Never Publishing 2017), the novella *Revenge of the Grand Narrative* (Quattro Books 2014), and of *Raise Some Shell* (ECW Press 2014), a cultural history of the Teenage Mutant Ninja Turtles. He is also a regular contributor to the popular culture analysis website *Overthinking It*. He lives in Toronto.